Praise for *Speak Gigantular*

"A liberatingly odd, seductive and fearless talent." Laline Paull, author of *The Bees*, shortlisted for the Bailey's Women's Prize for Fiction.

"Okojie delves into the painful, the unsayable, the unknowable. Her prose is precise and illuminating: love and loneliness are recurrent themes." Bernardine Evaristo, *The Guardian*

"Speak Gigantular is a work of rare confidence, luminous imagery and full of hidden sharp edges. There are few things that bring greater joy in reading than coming upon a talent so delightful, so penetrating, so scandalous. Okojie's stories are magical in all the most interesting senses of that word: devious, enthralling, unexpected." Nina Allan, winner of the Grand Prix de l'Imaginaire.

"A beautiful, sombre collection with deep shadows and dazzling highlights." *Mslexia*

"Each story featured is original, dark and with a witty but dark humour which disturbs and forces the reader to question exactly what a social norm is. This is fiction at its best, enacting change, driving the reader to act and it is spectac┄┄" *The Reading Pautort*

Praise for Irenosen Okojie

"A wonderful, richly drawn novel, cleverly juxtaposing scenes from everyday London with African folklore and mysticism." Joanne Harris

"A stunningly well written book, juggling different timescales with great skill. Benin itself is vividly imagined in a historical narrative that runs in parallel with the contemporary London one. It is a wonderful novel." Simon Brett

"A bittersweet story uniting different traditions of narrative to create a whole new geography of the imagination." Michele Roberts, Betty Trask Award judge

"Vital, vivid, witty, truthful..." Maggie Gee, *The Observer*

"Split between contemporary London and 19th-century West Africa, *Butterfly Fish* is a debut novel with an epic scope... The novel's strength is its ability to make the abstract concrete." *Oliver Zarandi, East End Review*

"One of the most original and innovative writers to emerge in many a year." Alex Wheatle, MBE

"*Butterfly Fish* is a novel of epic proportions... From sentence to sentence, Okojie conjures up acutely observed, beautifully-worded metaphors that resonate and delight... I fully expect to see *Butterfly Fish* on many an award nomination list. It is a fascinating read, and one I highly recommend." Yvvette Edwards (author of *A Cupboard Full of Coats*, longlisted for the Man Booker Prize)

"Her West African heritage is richly spun into her novel *Butterfly Fish*... The tale is peppered with moments of magical surrealism: a glass bottle shattering on a South London street to release two tiny scurrying figures into the night; a butterfly fish bursts into a local pool and belches a portentous brass key... The lyrical prose brings poignancy to the familiar London landscape." Samuel Fishwick, *Evening Standard*

"This is a very accomplished and colourful debut novel by a Nigerian-born English writer... Okojie tells not only a superbly well-written complex story of intertwining lives but uses a wonderfully colourful language and brings in Nigerian story-telling, myths and strange creatures, all of which make her English-based story more otherworldly. Okojie is clearly going to be an author to watch." John Alvey, *The Modern Blog*

"*Butterfly Fish* is a powerful novel of love, hope and loss written in Irenosen's unique and compelling style." *Greenacre Writers*

"Seriously unique and imaginative." Diana Evans, author of *26a* and winner of the Orange Prize

"A very able writer who has the gift of being able to paint the very picture that she is speaking of. Her writing has energy and her descriptions are full of flavour." Ashley Rose Scantlebury, *True Africa*

"Enchanting readers with the eloquence of a griot, Irenosen Okojie's début novel *Butterfly Fish* brings to life the magic of storytelling. In a spellbinding saga of love, deceit, guilt and atonement, it tells of the scourge of the sins of the ancestors upon the coming generation... The author's voice relates the ensuing drama with a gracious absence, bestowing to her characters' independence and authenticity. With a daring and distinctive tone, Irenosen is without a doubt a fresh addition to contemporary African fiction. *Butterfly Fish* is a dark and mesmerizing adventure packed with bittersweet delights. This is one of my personal favourites this summer. I highly recommend it." *Afrikult.com*

Speak Gigantular

by

Irenosen Okojie

JACARANDA

First published in Great Britain 2016 by
Jacaranda Books Art Music Ltd
Unit 304 Metal Box Factory
30 Great Guildford Street,
London SE1 0HS
www.jacarandabooksartmusic.co.uk

A CIP catalogue record for this book is available from the British
Library

ISBN: 978-1-909762-29-9
eISBN: 978-1-909762-46-6

Printed and bound in Great Britain
by CPI Group (UK) Ltd, Croydon, CR0 4YY

To Mum, Dad, Amen, Ota and Iredia, much love always.

To all the misfits who dare to tilt worlds.

Contents

Gunk

Gunk is a term in mereology for any whole whose parts all have further proper parts.

Get up. Try to hold your world. You can't. You let it slip. I know your world; car horns, aspiration, language, screaming traffic lights, spies. I see you. Your thick hair is overgrown, run an afro comb through it. Your wiry frame is still poised to move in sleep, to change shape at the edges of iodine stained misfortunes. I showed you how to plant, how to sow seeds in concrete, yet your seeds don't grow. I demonstrated ways to sheathe knives in skin, yet you only injure yourself. Boy, you don't fly. You don't appreciate flight. You just want to prove what a waste of space you are.

Stop trembling in the fucking corner. Don't pick up that medicine. They numb you, sedate you, curtail your potential. Don't follow the script. You weren't designed for this.

It's a set up. The system is fucking rigged. Your enemies plotted against you, danced on platforms in the sky, taunted you with disguises, reached into the chests of people you used to know. You rage because this city has broken you. This world has sucked your resolve through a pit. You rage because everything is a lie. Choice is an illusion. Its sibling conformity met you at the airport. Boy, you stepped into his fucking embrace proving what a waste of space you are. His smile made you forget your mother tongue while she battled the elements on your behalf, changing gears on any given day.

Remember Corrine? You told her coffee skin your secrets. She laughed, curved her wide mouth down to catch. You buried your face in her afro, travelled through it. You destroyed each other then came up for air. You watched her fly down the street engulfed in blue flames. A small universe spilled from her bag; notebook, pen, Vaseline, keys, items to trace on the scratched table when fear arrived with some creature's hind legs.

Your pity stinks. Stop cowering in the corner. Stop crawling naked on top of that wardrobe. You can't reinvent yourself from contained heights.

Darkness motivates men, mobilises armies. Use it. You are a warrior. Show me your roar. People are scared of your power, frightened of what you can do with it.

Once you wanted to be an engineer. Instead, those dreams drowned in the Thames. Instead, you walked off construction sites breathing sawdust. Instead, you avoided eye contact more so than usual. Instead, you resisted the urge to carry your internally bleeding head on public transport.

Follow my lead. Use those memories as lamps to see through your rooms. Nobody cares here. Footsteps on the stairs outside don't pause at this door. The carnival whistle hanging on the dented hallway wall waits for a cry that left you at birth to fill it. Your mobile phone stopped ringing. It's just you and me. You don't have any tricks. You just keep showing what a waste of space you are. You want to pick up that old taekwondo trophy and smash me to pieces. You can't. I gave you DNA.

These extras we programme ourselves to think are necessary—family, friends, jobs, love, companionship—these sentiments weakening us only serve as cushions to soften the inevitable blow. You'll die one day. Look around you, this is really it. Scraping pennies together so often it's become a past time, rummaging for money inside the sofa. Cracks in the ceiling, the floor that's turned to quicksand. No cash to charge the electricity, your fridge door opening to reveal half a yoghurt, one-day-old kebab. This unending humiliation of you to yourself facilitates nothing.

The couple next door were once in love. Now, you hear plates smashing, arguments fuelled by alcohol, the ripping of each other's carcasses, their misguided notions of loyalty. You watch their ugly Bombay cat skulking outside trying to trace where it pissed over the remedy for doomed lovers rising through cold soil.

You sit by this window looking out, hoping for answers. Boy, I gave you answers. If you weren't so busy showing what a waste of space you are, you'd remember. Your enemies are everywhere. They want to destroy you with fear. Don't let them do it. Don't be a puppet. I taught you better. I showed you better. I schooled you better. Don't be a victim. This is what a victim looks like. This is what you look like. Don't look like that. Didn't I teach you how they operate? Didn't I tell you how you're conditioned? Don't swallow what they're shoving down your throat. It costs them nothing. Didn't I teach you about currencies that can't be seen with the naked eye? Yet there you go proving what a waste of space you are.

Are you a small country? Are you a fucking island? Don't let your enemies conquer you. Don't let them limit you. Don't let them gag you. Don't let them buy your cooperation with their sleight of hand. Didn't I give you ammunition? Didn't we sharpen our tools? Didn't we aim for our bullseye from every possible angle, every feasible position? Yet there you lay trying to show what a waste of space you are.

Don't make me transform. Don't make me reconfigure.

I carried you.

I bled for you.

I suffered for you.

Stay close to me, listen. Every word I say to you is true.

Fuck governments.

Fuck systems.

Fuck everything that tells you if you're good you'll be valued.

Somebody always has to pay.

Make people pay.

We've paid enough.

Open your eyes. Get up from that bottom.

Son, this is the skin I'm leaving you with.

This is how to wear it comfortably.

This is how to camouflage when you need to.

This is how to start a war.

Remember: It's your world now.

Animal Parts

Henri Thomsen lived in the Danish town of Frederiksberg near Copenhagen. At ten-years-old he possessed one distinguishing feature; a long furry grey tail. The tail sprouted above his buttocks and through the hole that his mother Ann had been forced to make in the seat of all his trousers. Otherwise he looked like an average boy, with a shaggy mop of light brown hair that hung down over his forehead, inquisitive blue eyes and deep dimples in his cheeks into which his mother Ann sank adoring kisses.

As Henri grew older it became increasingly apparent that Ann was not going to be able to keep his tail a secret from the townsfolk. As uninhibited and unashamed as any child should be, Henri ran with oblivious abandon, not aware that words were forming against him, even at his tender young age. That minds were closing firmly, decidedly, and that he was not destined to enjoy his worry-free existence much beyond his early childhood years.

Strange things happened in the town now and again. Like the winter all the statues heads had gone missing, only to appear on the rooftops weeks later, one side of their faces collapsed while a splintered blue light flickered in their sockets. In the beginning, people thought Henri and his furry grey tail was some sort of joke. "Have you seen that Thomsen boy?" The town gossips ignorant spite-filled words went from door to door carried by the wind. "Wish he'd take that stupid costume off." The more they voiced their ugly opinions, the harder their stance on Henri became.

Across town Jorgen had spent the day finishing the tree house he'd invested hours into, outside of his job checking tickets on the ferries. When he heard the wind rustle and the words made their way to his ears.

"A freak," they said, "an abomination that needed to be locked away for the safety of everyone." When the voices of the two postmen gossiping about the boy with the tail caught his attention, Jorgen almost smashed a hammer through the left corner of the small picture frame he was hanging. "Who knew what diseases he was carrying? Why should they be put at risk?"

Jorgen listened, intrigued. His lazy left eye began to turn like green die spinning in static. Knowing how it felt to be slightly different from people, a shot of anger spread through his blood. He listened until their voices petered off.

That evening, Jorgen undressed to find a small, blue ball of light darting around under his skin. Absentmindedly, he picked up from his bedside dresser the small hammer he had been using earlier that day, repeatedly smacking it into his body, trying unsuccessfully to pin the blue ball frenetically travelling over his limbs. During the night the town's residents slept fitfully, the sky above their beds black like the tea that darkened their tongues.

As a baby, Henri's tail was a pearly stub, barely visible under his pale, white skin. Once he started growing so did the tail. At aged three, it shot out thick and strong. Ann, spellbound, watched him from her bedroom, in the bathroom, the hallway, everywhere; horrified, fascinated, trying to identify the smell of her own corrosive fear. It was a feeling she associated with the town and its inhabitants, even though she had been born there and had grown up among the very same people and strange occurrences.

Shortly after his birth, Ann took Henri to see the doctor for his well-baby check up. As she changed Henri, the last thing she worried about was her appearance. Rolling up the sleeves of her checked shirt, she tied her hair into a haphazard golden knot and scooped him up from his bed, hurriedly heading out the door. Ann was a pretty woman but the strain of worrying about Henri had slowly taken its toll, giving her a slightly harassed look. There was no man around to reassure her or hold her hands down when in utter frustration she clawed out fine clumps of hair from her head.

They'd trudged up to the local doctor, a dark navy blanket wrapped around Henri to cover his tail.

Later, she parted company with the doctor more confused. He couldn't tell her why her son had a tail; he assumed it must be some form of mutation. The boy was perfectly healthy otherwise and not in any danger. He recommended going to the hospital in Copenhagen for further tests. No. Ann had been adamant, she didn't want Henri being prodded and experimented on. Deep down, she knew all of that would have come to nothing.

At home she grabbed a nondescript grey file of newspaper clippings from under the bed; stories of unusual people from around the world; A baby born in India with multiple sets of lower limbs who the locals believed was the reincarnation of one of their most revered Gods. A woman whose spine had overgrown and protruded through her skin like the dorsal vertebra of an ancient mythic creature. Her hand stilled over the file. Soon, she would start sharing these tales with Henri. She felt reassured somehow that these strangers had begun to talk to her from the shadowy space beneath her bed.

As time passed, Henri became the one constant in her life. He kept her company while from home she ran a tiny cottage business, making jams that she sold to the townsfolk and local shops. She was almost as famous for her jams as she was for her son. Aware of the provincial tastes of the townspeople, Ann would fold in exotic flavours into her sweet fruit as it cooked. The most popular ones were chocolate and banana, almond and orange, and apricot with vanilla. She attended to them in the small cosy kitchen of her home, adding a variety of spices, a dash of nutmeg and cinnamon and sometimes even sea salt. Henri would proudly hold the jars while she filled them with the cooled fruit, his tail gently wagging. She would label them carefully using brightly coloured paper she allowed him to stick on the jars.

They made deliveries in her old turquoise Fiat 500 which sputtered loudly along the town's quaint roads, so that people always heard them coming. They were reliable Ann and Henri, team jam procurers extraordinaire. They mostly delivered on time. On the doorsteps, rifling through the variety of jeweled toned, sweet-smelling jars in Ann's basket people would often ask Henri if he knew his mother's secret ingredient, staring at the jars as though sinister things lurked behind the sweetness. These times were their main interactions with the community and a social lifeline for Henri. Ann rarely had visitors to her home. Occasionally in winter when he made his rounds, Hans the mill operator would drop wood by the house, face ruddy, full red beard unkempt, smiling at Ann as if he was the bearer of known truths. Other than him, no-one came.

At night Ann listened to her mother's old radio with the faulty knob that came off if you gripped it too enthusiastically. Now and again, she swore she could hear her mother's crisp, flat voice dispatching parental advice between frequencies.

During these moments, sharp pains hit her chest. Curling up into a ball, she could barely breathe. What had she done? What would become of her son? The loneliness and desire for a child before him had been all-consuming. Were anything ever to happen to her, she did not trust the town to take care of her son, but the world out there beyond it was even more frightening.

Eleven years prior to Henri's birth, a stranger had turned up at Ann's door. When Ann had heard the knock at the door she first thought it was one of her neighbours and she had found herself silently wishing it was the one she liked, as opposed to the obnoxious hellion who lived directly across from her. Upon opening the door, Ann saw no-one she recognised. Standing before her as if she had intentionally arrived at the address, although Ann had no knowledge of her, was a woman with a sharp black bob and an accent Ann couldn't place. Feline looking, she had perfectly symmetrical features and a seductive air about her. Her full red mouth blew misty air into Ann's face. Her long, slender fingers curled. Dark, almond shaped eyes glinted. She wore black jeans paired with a white polo neck.

The woman spoke directly at Ann in a firm measured tone. She said in a throaty voice that her car had broken down at the top of the road and asked if she could use her phone to call someone for help. The woman wore an electronic bracelet on her wrist that flickered blue light as she languidly waved her hands in emphasis, almost as if she was bored. Ann noticed small, circular blue blotches on her right arm.

Before Ann knew it, she was pulling the woman in from the cold and the heavily falling snow. Tall and lean, the woman shook snow off her boots, then trailed behind Ann into the sitting area where the fire blazed and a nearly empty bottle of scotch stood on the mantelpiece. She noticed Ann's red-rimmed eyes, her tear streaked cheeks.

"Bad timing?" she asked in a cool but empathic tone. "I won't keep you."

The alcohol she'd consumed made Ann feel light-headed, although she was happy to have company.

The woman tucked strands of hair behind her right ear. For the first time, Ann spotted a large birthmark that had been obscured by her hair. It was blue, lotus shaped. She'd never seen a blue scar before. She tried not to stare. The flaw made the woman appealing and somehow more approachable. Ann had always admired physical differences that gave people an air of uniqueness.

"What's brought you to Frederiksberg? What do you do? I make jams," Ann said, slightly embarrassed at her eagerness for conversation.

The stranger smiled patiently, rubbed her hands by the fire. "I procure unusual things for people, which means I travel extensively to all sorts of places. Have you always wanted to be in the cottage industry?" the woman asked.

Ann held her gaze. There was a kindness there and genuine interest she had not expected. Ann was used to very few people paying her any attention.

"I enjoy making jams. I'm good at it. And, it may not sound ambitious but I've always wanted to be a mother. I like children you see," Ann answered.

"Yes, I find that helps," the woman quipped. They both laughed. This stranger had a way about her, a warmth that wasn't immediately apparent.

The woman blew her breath against her fingers. "Being a mother must be special. I say that because I never knew my mother. I have a feeling your child will know you well."

Ann flushed, pleased at the compliment. The stranger

reached for a photograph of Ann and with an older woman on the mantelpiece.

"Is this your mother?" she asked.

Ann nodded.

They had been canoeing that day. In the picture she and her mother stood by large rocks laughing, wet from the water, surrounded by rolling mountains shrouded in mist. A cabin sat on a mountain in the distance. Moments before, their canoe had tossed over sending them into thrashing waters. At the time, for a brief moment in the water, Ann had considered holding her mother down beneath the swirling surface, silencing her cruel taunts forever.

"You're just like your father," her mother Begitta used to say. "You're weak, there's no place in the world for weaklings, Ann." Ann imagined what it would be like to never hear those words again, briefly entering the rushing void in which only her mother's silence remained. But then the moment passed.

On the journey back home in the car, as her mother talked, all Ann could see was white water steadily cresting over her mother's flapping pink tongue.

The stranger did not comment on the photo, instead she smoothed her hair back, turned to Ann and asked, "Is there someone I can call?"

"Oh! Of course. Let me ring Dieter," Ann offered. "He has a truck. It rarely gives him trouble. He's a mechanic you see."

The women drank ginger tea while they waited for Dieter. When he arrived, brusque and slightly irritated at having been dragged out of his home that late in the evening, the stranger held Ann's hands, smiling crookedly. "Impossible things happen all the time, Ann," she said. Then she swept out behind Dieter, her long legs disappearing through the front door, into the unforgiving weather.

After she left all that Ann recalled was the woman's

long, slender fingers, as they had held Ann's own hands; their coolness and yet their kindness. Stumbling a little by the fireplace, she noticed a plain white business card slipped into the photo frame on the mantle. *Love Larry Inc.* it read in unfussy black text. *Sperm donor bank.* Ann removed the card slowly, as if hypnotized. Her mouth went dry. Her heartbeat quickened.

Outside, gates rattled. She could hear the crunch of tires in snow, a whistle trapped in a keyhole somewhere that belonged to her. Standing there alone, drunk and feeling pathetic, she thought about her mother Begitta, reliving the car accident that had killed her. She imagined walking out into the road and leaping through someone's windscreen, reaching for her mother's talking, battered head through the glass.

She held the card up to the light. *Love Larry Inc.* How bizarre. She cried softly thinking of Begitta and of the stranger's red mouth, plump like ripe fruit and all the secrets it took with it into the crevices of winter.

Ann heard about the town's Neighbourhood Watch gathering through a customer. She had not received the invitation in the usual way; a folded sheaf of printed eggshell-coloured paper slipped into her letter box. It was only on the night, arriving soaked from the heavy rain and loitering at the back of the main playhouse room which doubled as a venue for local activities that she realised the meeting was about Henri. Her son had become the main item on their agenda. One by one, people she knew as neighbours and customers stood in the half-filled space to air their concerns, emboldened by their numbers and common small mindedness. Their palpable fear took the shape of a virus.

"What about our children? I don't want that… that thing to turn on any of my girls one day," Gustav said. A man she had gone to school with and comforted when his wife Elaina had died from leukemia.

"We have a right to know where he came from, what he is. Ann is too secretive. I don't trust her. She doesn't have our best interests at heart; if she did they'd leave," Marie, the town seamstress, interjected. She carried a needle beneath her tongue. Her hands fluttered nervously, ready to depart, to catch the things she disapproved of in angles of light.

"What if it... *he*'s carrying diseases?" Paulina asked. A painter who had lost part of her memory several years back, she could walk into a scene from her past mid-conversation. "Maybe he needs to be quarantined," she continued.

Enraged, Ann's voice took over. "You're the ones who need to be quarantined!" Ann spat. "He's just a boy. He's innocent."

Murmurs shot through the crowd sucking the air out of the room. Each adjusted their bodies to look at her.

"This is our home," Ann said. "We're not going anywhere." Her voice trembled. The thin needle beneath Marie's tongue pricked holes in the quiet that followed. Ann left.

Back out in the rain, she molded their betrayal with small movements. Ugly pulped features fighting for a reassembling governed the night. Ann felt hollow, as though they'd eaten her defenses to grow back the skin on their faces. She shrieked in anger, frustration. The only response was the squish of water in her boots.

Walking back, her mind fixated on the eight-limbed baby in India and the extremely hairy circus man from Peru. She thought about this man all the way home, wondering what had become of him.

Ann decided to take Henri to the cabin in Mons Klint for his eighth birthday, as her mother had done for her. It was a rite of passage that had been in their family for generations. Her hands fidgeted at the wheel. She took deep breaths starting the engine, checking the side mirrors nervously. She'd packed enough for three days, including two Dr. Seuss books and a copy of Hans Christian Anderson's *Fairy Tales*, which Henri loved. Once, he'd told her he wished he could enter those worlds and discover other people like him. There, he didn't think he'd be asked why he was dressed for Halloween early.

Henri had never left Frederiksberg. The trip excited him. As he entered their little blue car a part of him worried who they may meet. What if they didn't like him or his mother? What if his tail frightened them? He had gotten used to the looks people gave him back home; curiousity, wonder, fear and sometimes outright dismay. There were a few kind people who were nice to him, several of Ann's customers gave him sweets, asked how he was. Some of the older ones had kindness in their eyes.

He enjoyed accompanying his mother on her rounds but he didn't tell Ann that sometimes he wondered what it was like to not have his tail, to be like other boys who appeared carefree, who didn't have to cut holes in their trousers to make room for a tail. It seemed he wasn't only making room for his tail, but other unknown things. He felt guilty having these thoughts. Ann would often say, "You're extraordinary, why would you want to be like everybody else?"

He knew if he mentioned these feelings she would worry. She'd start doing the thing that set his teeth on edge, pulling out clumps of hair in frustration. He never knew what the right response was when she got like that. He'd sit in his room running a hand over the length of his tail, eyes watering, trying to calculate the weight of it, imagining it spinning in the sky over the buildings of the town before landing unceremoniously on doorsteps.

He watched his tail in mirrors around the house, while it

floated slick and wet in the bath. He trimmed a little fur off it; spread the thick hairs on his white sheet, where they lay grey against the starkness. He took to secretly flicking through newspapers and magazines to see if there was anybody like him. Ann wouldn't let him watch TV, claiming it corrupted the mind, that once it was set in motion, it couldn't be undone. He looked up the word undone in Ann's dictionary. It meant *incomplete, not tied or fastened*. The word flashed in his mind.

He'd have to attend school soon. The thought brought a stone of dread to his throat. Suddenly the car stalled. Ann fumbled with the keys. A feeling of sickness and resentment crept into his chest. His stomach lurched.

They drove for a few hours under a grey sky. Ann had forgotten parts of the route so they got lost now and again, stopping on remote roads to ask passing drivers for directions. Henri played his part, flagging cars down using his bright, orange drawing book. Back on their way again, he busied himself sketching a father figure with a tail and an injured blue deer. He drew the father in detail; wearing a dapper tweed jacket, holding a passport to wander hidden worlds, to see things the average eye would miss. The father pointed at the deer, instructing it. Above the picture, Henri scribbled the word *Speak*.

Their first day there, Ann taught Henri how to pitch a tent. The wind knocked it over so they pitched it again, laughing. She took him fishing, amused as he held his tongue up to the bait. On the second day they climbed the cliffs slowly, steadily towards the blue man Ann had promised was waiting with a gift but who turned out to be just an engraving on one damp wall.

She was glad they were away from the eyes of others just for a little while, happy to teach him things she was scared she might one day lose the will to do. Finally, she took him to the waters where the shape of a tossed canoe still lingered. Some would have found it alarming that Ann spent several hours in the same spot where she'd considered drowning her own mother, teaching her son how to hold his breath underwater.

Shivering, she watched his little legs kicking, arms and head breaking the surface gasping, "How long do we have to do this for?"

They kept at it together. She held his hand underwater, in the cold blue even when she felt the brush of something inside tugging them. She wondered if they'd become sacrifices to the undertow, if her ghosts would swap their irises for blind eyes. Even when all the eels and fish wielded red mouths, swimming aggressively towards them, they practiced until Henri could hold his breath counting to thirty. Afterwards on the bank, holding him tightly, she promised to buy him a telescope. She told him that she'd taught him that lesson because he would need it. The drive home was one of quiet comfort.

Henri's first day at school had been stressful for Ann. That morning, he stood before her in his black trousers and the white shirt she'd ironed three times. His shoes were polished to a high shine and his tail was tucked inside his trousers.

When they arrived at the large black school gates, she ushered him in firmly. On the steps, surrounded by excited, yapping children whom Ann imagined carried soft rag toys in their small rucksacks, he tentatively turned to look at her one last time, searching for something in her expression. She waved enthusiastically, feeling fresh tears emerging, rubbing the car keys with shaking fingers.

By late afternoon, she received a call from the secretary whose tone was brisk and impersonal asking her to come to the school. Arriving back at the school, she found Henri in the lobby, kicking the shiny floor with restrained anger, a pained expression on his face. The hours had been unkind; ripping buttons from his pristine, thrice-ironed shirt, sullying it with food and dirt. There were scratches on his forehead, a small bruise on his right cheek. His hair smelled of urine, the back of his trousers was ripped open and his tail stuck out, exposed once and for all to see.

"What happened?" she sank down, grabbing his shoulders. "Who did this to you?"

He shook his head and begged urgently, "Please let's go home."

Henri was convinced something was wrong with his mother. He began to notice small clumps of hair dotted around the house. The middle part of her head was now almost completely bald. He found himself measuring it with small internal fingers, tracing the growing pale patch, watching it suspiciously as though it was an entry point to frightening things she couldn't bring herself to tell him.

She had lost interest in cooking, so Henri made her jam sandwiches, simple meals from cold cuts of meat and whatever else he found rummaging through the kitchen cupboards. She listened to her radio obsessively. Now and again, he caught her dancing wildly in the evenings. Blasting the radio, she flung her body around, as if wanting to disappear through its movements. Other occasions, she sat up quietly in her bed, the radio low, the lamplight on, a thumbed novel on her dresser, listening intensely for something.

Henri felt scared, sad and alone. He felt responsible somehow for Ann's behaviour but he didn't know what to do. Most people in the town kept away from them. He knew it was because of his tail. Ann had no real friends. He realised this was what people meant by being lonely. He looked the word up in the pocket dictionary Ann kept on her bedroom bookshelf.

Loneliness: the quality of being unfrequented and remote; forsakenness, abandonment, rejection.

Henri thought loneliness was possibly the worst thing in the world.

One morning, Ann had set two glasses on the mantle piece, lit the fire and changed out of her dressing gown. Pacing before the fireplace, she muttered, "I'm waiting for someone" while anxiously wringing her hands. "She never told me this could happen. She never warned me!" Her voice was sharp, accusatory. It froze his insides.

Hours later, the second glass was still untouched. The woman, whoever she was to his mother, never came.

Henri began walking to school by himself. Ann had become tired all the time, preferring to lie down in her room. En route to school that morning, the feeling of drowning, of doom was overwhelming. Ann appeared to him randomly along the way, a hologram in the cold, frantically tugging out clumps of hair, dropping them on the ground. They twitched, small hairy animals in the snow.

At lunch time, Henri hid in the last toilet cubicle as the afternoon bell rang. He'd run on instinct, tripping along the way. Passing a white sink with a crack in it, he scrambled for safety behind the grey toilet door. He sat with his back against the wall, knees up, trying to hold himself still. He imagined disappearing through the crack in the sink, emerging through the other side with a small scar on his chest and without his tail which had been carefully hidden inside his trousers, tucked and flattened.

He heard the sound of car tires pulling away in the snow, children laughing, scattering out into the playground. Other children laughed, played, were happy. These things felt foreign to Henri. The panic rose inside him. His breaths became short and fast. His heart raced. A burning sensation spread in his throat as he realised he'd forgotten to lock the cubicle door. He reached out to slide the lock into the catch, hand trembling. It was jammed, damaged from the door being kicked in.

Oh God, Henri thought as footsteps approached in the hall, *please don't let them come in. Please let them pass.*

His arm sank to the ground. The lock caught on his tongue mockingly. He pulled his small, brown school bag closer as if getting comfort from it, clinging to the strap. There was nothing inside it he could use to defend himself, except a fork he'd grabbed from the kitchen counter at home, sticky with maple syrup.

He closed his eyes unable to move, to scream, fear thick in his mouth. He saw the fork spinning at the bottom of the bag, caught in the moments his heart sank and died each day before swelling and beating again. A sharp pain shot through his chest to his tail. He wished he had a father, a brother. They would know what to do. Why didn't he know what to do? He opened the bag, grabbing the fork. He closed his eyes.

The main toilet door swung open followed by a high laugh he recognised, that somehow seemed disembodied from the small frame it belonged to, reaching him ahead of the pack. His grip on the fork tightened. Cold sweat ran down his back. The footsteps were so close he could trace them with the fork, his silvery inadequate weapon. The cubicle door swung open slowly, sending a shiver through him. His fork clattered pathetically to the floor. Somebody flushed another toilet before leaving quickly. His tormentor Christoff stood in the doorway; blonde, cherubic, cruel. He held an opened tin can in his hands, flanked by two other boys sharing an energy that crackled, grinning at each other excitedly. Christoff held the can to him as though it was a peace offering. The smell from it was rotten, acrid.

"Why won't you come and eat with us, Henri? Pets eat when their owners tell them to. I've brought you some dog food," Christoff said.

The other boys laughed. Christoff passed the can to the boy on his left who kept glancing at the door. Christoff kicked him in the face. It came so suddenly, Henri had no time to prepare for the pain, the ringing in his ears, the crack and thud that echoed between the breathing of boys. He reached out, pleading blindly, silently with his left arm. Tears stung his eyes. Christoff fished out a pair of black scissors from his pocket as the other boys dragged him out.

"Show us your tail," they chorused like a small warped choir.

Henri shook his head defiantly, gulping as Christoff waved the scissors, catching bits of light. His thoughts bled into one stunted footstep limping as it tried to cross the clatter of a fork, the sinewy gleam of scissor blades. Henri's body shook, his nose hurt, he felt light-headed. The boys were interchangeable to him. They all spoke with one voice, Christoff's. Christoff edged closer, enjoying the fear in Henri's eyes. A tubby child with one lazy eye, he relished tormenting a boy more different than anybody he'd ever seen. He spat in Henri's face.

"What are you?" Christoff asked, fascinated. "My mother says you shouldn't be here."

Henri turned his head away, struggling as the other two boys held his arms back. He looked up at the swirls of circular patterns on the white ceiling desperate for an exit. He wished he hadn't gotten out of bed that morning. He wished he'd never left the safety of home. He wished he'd never been born.

The boys turned him over. Christoff cut into his trousers,

yanking his tail out. They turned him over again. Christoff's cheeks were pink, his blue eyes wild.

He picked up the can of dog food, dramatically announcing, "We can't eat until you've eaten."

Henri desperately wished someone would burst in to rescue him but nobody came. They appeared to be apart from everything else, a limb of time that had fractured from it, operating without its consent. Christoff grabbed the fork from the floor. One boy shoved Henri's face into the can of dog food, the open lid like another mouth cutting him just above his lip. Its rotten scent filled his nostrils.

"Eat or we won't leave," Christoff instructed. Smiling, exchanging a look with the others, he scooped a forkful of jellied lump from the can, holding it up to Henri's lips. Henri opened his mouth reluctantly. Tears ran down his cheeks as forkful after forkful Christoff fed him until only a quarter of it was left. Henri gagged numerous times, spittle shooting from his lips, he coughed, spluttered. Each time as punishment he was force-fed more. The boys emptied the remainder of the food inside his bag, shoving the can and fork in. They tried to set his tail on fire using matchsticks, only to be interrupted by the ringing of another bell.

After they left, Henri grabbed his bag. He got to his feet unsteadily, slowly and dejectedly walking towards the door. On the other side, Marlena, the girl he had made a bracelet for the other week, was waiting in the hallway. Her pixie-like face was flushed, worried.

"Are you okay?" she asked.

Oh God, Henri thought, *she heard everything*. And the smell. He knew it by the way she caught his eye before looking away guiltily, as she unconsciously sent a finger just beneath her nose.

In that moment, he wanted to die. He wanted to disappear.

He hated being different. His mother had lied. He wasn't special. He was cursed.

He ran, leaving Marlena clutching smoke from his tail. He bolted down the hall, past the reception and out through the gates. He opened his bag, found the fork that had betrayed him and flung it at the school. He hoped it would do the one thing he wanted, uproot it as if by magic, leaving behind a chasm in its place.

That night he couldn't sleep. The tin canned mouth appeared in his doorway making the sound of a toilet flushing. Henri's nostrils filled with the scent of dog food again. He started trembling. The mouth told him he was due his next set of injuries. He followed it out into the cold and the dark on all fours. He met the night with his heart pounding, his pajama bottoms damp with piss. Small rockets on it threatened to take off powered by urine and heartache. A baptism of snow fell on his skin, unable to remove the sting of humiliation. Henri crawled as the mouth expanded. He hated himself, hated his tail. He crawled because he deserved it.

In the morning, Ann found him in a neighbour's yard, half naked with scratches on his thighs. He had one bloodshot eye and was crying into an empty can of dog food.

For three months Henri's tormentors continued. The teachers did nothing. The children said nothing. Their silence conspired against him. Until one afternoon, after arriving home from school, he burst through their kitchen ahead of Ann who had been emptying the freezer. He grabbed a knife. Tears streamed down his face. "Cut it off, Mama!"

"No, calm down, please," she said, trying to swallow the dread rising.

"I'm a freak! Cut it off or I will," he screamed, face red eyes shining dangerously.

"Henri, give me the knife." She set down a pack of frozen peas on the counter slowly.

"No, you did this to me. I HATE YOU! This is all your fault." He pointed the knife at her. The cold kitchen echoed his words. *All your fault.* The bread crumbs on the chopping board lingered close to the edge, as though they would fall into the gulf between them that had been steadily forming.

Suddenly the tap dripping sounded louder than a close range gunshot. She dived for her son. They wrestled on the floor. He wriggled his body, raising the knife. She grabbed his stomach; he kicked her in the face, a jolt of electricity travelled to her brain. She let go, watching him vanish through the door.

"Fine," she yelled, standing, breath ragged, running up the stairs to find him before her bedroom mirror with his trousers off.

"Okay," she said, "I can't bear to see you like this anymore." Her shoulders sank, she smoothed the flowery duvet down.

"Please don't send me back to that school, promise?" he asked.

She sighed, stilled her trembling body. In her mind's eye she saw the procession of rag dolls covered in blood coming towards them, the sound of school gates opening a symphony in the background.

"I promise." She grabbed a small, white sunken pillow from her bed.

It was after dinner by the time Ann decided she could no longer delay the inevitable. The fire crackled in the living room. Stacked, chopped logs taunted her. The axe beside them cut the edges of the silence.

She grabbed the axe, took Henri into the kitchen thinking

that the equation of a boy, his mother and an axe had several outcomes. She spread an old black paint-stained sheet over the table. Henri sat on it biting down on the pillow. She remembered being pregnant. How she'd ran her hands over her belly each morning, amazed at its growth, its widening circumference. She recalled listening to the radio at nights intensely, hearing something travelling through the frequency to deliver a message to the child inside her and when she held Henri for the first time and he looked her in the eye blinking gunk away, she knew that message had been delivered, that he had entered her womb before.

After he was born, sometimes she found herself holding the *Love Larry Inc.* card, starring at it in wonder, grateful that it had satisfied the type of longing and loneliness a woman who craved a child knew only for another kind to sprout up in its place. In those dark, empty days before Henri came, Ann had followed the echoes of a child's laughter through the house, arms outstretched, heart thudding. Long before Henri crawled towards her at six months old, tail protruding from his soiled diaper, a dangerous light in his iris spreading until she thought his right eye changed colour.

Ann imagined Henri's tail was wood, a dead thing. Sweat popped on her brow. She counted to ten slowly inside, testing the weight of the axe, waiting for something to change her mind. She brought it down in a firm stroke. Something shattered behind her eyes, scattering into the grainy static. Henri's face went white, he grimaced, the pillow dropped.

"I'm sorry I've been a bad mother," she said, her head now almost completely shorn gleamed ominously, the sprigs of hair giving her a demented look. She steadied her left hand on the table, lifted the axe with her right, smashing it down over her wrist with all the strength she could muster. She screamed. Henri stared, horrified. The axe fell to the floor with a thud. Blood covered her clothes. The pain was so intense Ann thought she would faint. She stumbled towards Henri, bleeding as he bled. Faces twisting, they watched his tail and her hand on the floor, spinning towards the axe in the warped silence as if for one more stroke of destruction.

Outtakes

The hot water bottle exploding on my leg was a bad omen.

At Paddington station, Balthazar sent me a text. Balthazar was my boyfriend of exactly one year. He was the interesting and good-looking father of two lovely girls. Elaborate stories wriggled out of his mouth like fluorescent, scaly fish. He had rumpled brown hair and green eyes. He didn't seem to own an iron. Always slightly dishevelled, he laughed through everything. If I'd told him one of my legs got bitten off by a crocodile he'd have said, "Oh hon! That's terrible! Want me to come and massage your stump?" *Soft chuckle, soft chuckle.*

In the beginning, he loved to say my name, Desiree; eventually he started calling me Desi for short. Balthazar knew something about everything, including octopus festivals, chortling volcanoes and placenta-eating women. He was a veritable talking, languid, brown-haired Wikipedia. He'd been to art school at Goldsmiths and when that didn't pan out, as is often the case with dreams of our youth, he settled into the role of a psychiatrist, an intelligent creature in a position of responsibility.

His text said: *Hon got something to tell you. Make sure you're standing somewhere quiet. xx*

The strap of my zebra-striped bag ate into my shoulder. I dropped it, vaguely registering a thud. I missed-called him. He called me back straight away, delivering a velvet-gloved blow as though it was some anecdote pulled out of a hat, a distant fanged thing that couldn't really touch us: "Ah, I've been sleeping with Tara."

What? No! Aloud I said, "Are you serious? Is this a joke?"

Although at first we'd been intimate, in the past six months Balthazar hadn't been able to get it up. No hard, throbbing, jerking, insatiable erection for me. No sir. I was practically a fucking nun in my late twenties. In that familiar, disconcerting unravelling that occurs when you receive bad news, I could only see me. People swirled around but I could only hear my heartbeat, my shallow breaths, I saw big grey brains curling, parting, and then reassembling into the silhouette of a woman.

"She's absolutely furious with me, she's been calling continuously!" he said.

"How long has this been going on?" I asked, leaning against the wall.

"About two weeks. Oh Desi, I'm so sorry, she's just… there. We're only compatible sexually. In every other way we're completely wrong for each other!"

"And why did you choose to tell me this now, Balthazar? Just as we're about to go to Tavira together? Don't you think that's cruel? Why not two days ago?"

"I just couldn't bear you not knowing, I'm sorry, I'd still like you to come with me."

"You're lucky I didn't already pay the train fare for Stroud!" I spat.

"I know," he said wearily.

"Do you really think I'd want to come with you now? You must be out of your fucking mind."

"Look, I really fancy you," he whined. "But there's a disconnect somewhere between us that's baffling. And the whole sexual thing… well it's a pain you know. Part of the reason I started sleeping with Tara was to prove to myself there wasn't something wrong with me. But how to tell you?"

"I'm not the one that can't get it up!" My voice sounded thin to my own ears, terse. I wanted to reach inside my head and stop it sending parts of the bomb to my chest, heart and throat.

"I'm sorry." His voice was a ghost now.

"What do you expect me to say? No, really? I'm getting off this line," I yelled, ignoring the concerned looks a few passersby threw my way.

I sat on my bag and watched people rush past, as if reading their faces would give me answers. Balthazar was occasionally unpredictable but I never suspected he would cheat. He was generous, thoughtful and attentive. I could not believe he had done it with Tara, the woman who lived doorsteps away from him, who he'd disparaged. She's a lunatic! She's been stalking me! I should have guessed, men are usually fucking or want to fuck women they dismiss as crazy. Tara lived out of a van like a wild, nomadic creature. She was the kind of woman that would dance around Stonehenge naked, stay in some eco-village with strangers, build giant composts, piss in buckets of hay and expect an internal revelation when the sun came up.

I was the opposite, dusky-skinned, creative and adventurous but I was a city girl, I barely owned the right pair of boots to traipse around the countryside for long walks, something Balthazar loved to do. Balthazar happily introduced me to friends and family while Tara climbed poles and windows to interrupt gatherings declaring her love. It was Shakespearean. I wasn't going to compete, not my style. Getting my own van and bandying about the British countryside in it which would never work because:

a) I'd freeze unless it was summer;

b) I'm bad at map reading so getting lost would be a frequent occurrence;

c) I'd be craving spicy food consistently;

d) No access to the internet might make me temporarily insane;

e) What if I accidently fell asleep having left the van door open and some creature ate me? This would be a genuine concern.

Me in a van travelling through the countryside equalled a series of calamities. There was nothing I wanted to do. I shifted my weight to the side. My appetite was gone, which meant only one thing: I was definitely upset.

The next day scalded leg in tow; I caught a flight to Lisbon while Balthazar travelled to Tavira with his ten-year-old daughter Alice. I figured I'd booked the time off work and still wanted to travel. Easy Jet didn't even serve a meal on flight. I have a small build but spend a lot of time thinking about food. At breakfast I start planning lunch, at lunch time I begin to imagine dinner. This cycle rarely deviated from its course.

In Lisbon I stayed at El Rancho, a hotel hidden in an ancient gothic building that looked nondescript from the outside. You had to go two floors up to find it, tucked away inside like the architectural equivalent of nesting boxes. Its glass doors parted if you clapped or waved. I pretended to flap as though I'd sprouted wings in the small metallic ancient lift that creaked all the way up as if it would get stuck in the ether. I flapped my new wings and the doors opened. The inside was comfortable and cosy. My room had a large, sprawling dark wooden bed, wide white windows, a cream coloured bathroom and satellite TV with some English speaking channels. The guy at reception was very friendly. He even told me where his favourite restaurant was.

The next morning, the friendly receptionist was replaced by a thin man with a ferret face and a pinched expression. I needed an adaptor plug to charge my mobile phone. He gave me clear directions. I told him my room was a little cold and he offered to turn the heating up while I was out.

I found myself on the narrow winding streets littered with quaint, tiny shops. After a jaunt that was almost fruitless, I bought an adaptor and returned to the hotel. I ate a sandwich, watched a couple of *Family Guy* episodes, sent a scathing text or two to Balthazar's apologetic ones, crashed for a bit.

By 3pm I decided to use the Internet room upstairs. I took my bankcards, my phone and I left my purse. I carried two 50 euro cents coins, locked my room door and spotted a scowling cleaner outside fiddling with towels. I handed my keys to the guy at reception and asked him to turn up my heating. Upstairs the machine required 1 euro coins specifically so I ran back down to get my purse. Within the space of five minutes my bed had been made, the receptionist had turned up the heating and my purse was missing.

"My purse has disappeared," I said, rushing up to him. "It's purple with a red rose on it. It was in my room and now it's gone!"

He looked at me blankly. "No, I have not seen this purse."

"Ask the cleaner!" I replied, my voice rising. They exchanged words in Portuguese. "Look I have two hundred euro in that purse, all the money I was carrying on me and now it's gone, whoever stole it is still in this hotel."

We went back to my room where they both pretended to help me look for it. I was furious. *You bastards*, I thought. *One of you is a thief checking for a purse you've stolen.* I was livid; my skin so warm the hot water bottle exploding on my leg seemed like a distant memory. I confronted the receptionist again.

"All I know is both of you went into that room within a couple of minutes and now my money's gone," I said, frowning at the unapologetic faces before me.

"I trust our staff more than I trust a stranger's words. They have worked here for many years. How do we know that you are not making this up to get out of paying your hotel bill?" the receptionist countered, his collar tight against his neck. He waved his arms as though conducting the scene.

"What?" I spat. "You are an imbecile. That is ridiculous. Why would I make this up? I'm a client in this hotel, a guest in your country and frankly your lack of sympathy is making me suspicious."

My God, these people were unbelievable. The cleaner with her lank black hair continued to look as though she had better things to do; the receptionist turned red with annoyance. The hotel manager, a short, chubby grey-haired patronizing bastard was called. I repeated my predicament and his response was: "This never happen in our hotel before! Your case is first, our staff are good people."

Yeah right. Motherfuckers!

"Besides," the hotel manager continued, smiling falsely with a kind of deadness in his eyes, "he said he didn't like that you gave him the key and asked him to turn your room temperature up. To him, the room was warm enough."

"Yes," the receptionist piped in. "To me the temperature was fine. If not for the cleaner being there I feel you would blame only me. I feel you are trying to frame me!"

"This is absolutely ridiculous." I was bordering on hysterical, afraid I would punch one of them any minute. "Who gives a shit whether you thought the room was warm enough or not? I'm a paying guest and it's my preference. What would I gain by framing you?"

They fiddled about, pointlessly checking my room again.

Fed up, I promised myself I'd go to the police. I left and spent three hours trawling the streets looking for another hotel. The hotels fell into two brackets, upscale and out of my budget or dumps I couldn't bear to subject myself to even for one night. By 8pm I gave up the search and went for dinner. I no longer wanted to see Lisbon. I knew it was childish but I blamed the city for my misfortune.

I sent Balthazar a text, since he was in Portugal too. He responded quickly: *Oh hon, sorry to hear that. Fuck 'em! Come and stay with us, plenty of room in this apartment and you don't need money here. xx*

I went back to my hotel room afterwards. I slept with one eye open, just in case the staff attempted to kill me.

I settled my account with the hotel the next morning and checked out. It was one of those bright hot days that made you grateful to be alive. I reported the crime to the *policia*. I was interviewed by an abrupt, strapping, bearded officer with a dented head. Throughout our exchange I fixated on how I could repair it for him.

I caught the metro to Oriente after asking a lovely Angolan man for directions. He insisted on accompanying me, carried my bags and everything. I was touched. We struggled to understand each other but the journey sped by with his engaging company. He had a handsome open face and his smile made me want to reveal things to him. His brown skin was smooth and beautiful, it was impossible not to stare at it. We swapped contact details.

At Oriente, I caught a coach to Faro; I was travelling to the back of beyond while lost segments of my life occupied the empty seats. In Faro, the train I took groaned down the track to Tavira. You could see green countryside lit with bright yellow flowers for miles.

On arrival, the train delivered a good number of passengers. Balthazar and Alice were holding hands on the platform; each a larger or miniature extension of the other. Alice wore a smile and a bright blue scarf fashioned in a sarong style over her clothes. In one hand she clutched a worn teddy, Bear Bear, whose nose had been bitten off. I gave her a hug and Balthazar a cooler greeting.

In the silver Yaris, I sat in the back with Alice, listening as she filled me in on their day at the beach. If Alice were a colour she'd be one that changed kaleidoscopically, first yellow, then blood red, then magenta. She was spirited, creative, intelligent and funny but also spoilt, snobbish, emotionally astute and manipulative. She had the uncanny ability to define people in that blunt, unpretentious way only children are capable of.

"Dad had this girlfriend before, Laura. All she ever said was 'fab' and 'brill'." This was said with what I imagined was the correct intonation in her voice and it made me laugh out loud.

Their apartment looked like an upscale granny flat, displays of china, weathered old-fashioned chairs, but it was spacious and comfortable. Alice turned the TV on; we watched the Hollywood channel which played terrible films on loop. Alice had me chuckling with her witty lines and funny antics. She did a perfect imitation of the Chipmunks and repeated fabricated conversations in song, Chipmunk-style. This drove Balthazar mad, but since she had an audience there was no stopping her. Watching his attempts to control his precocious child was amusing.

By 8pm we were starving and wandered over to Balthazar's favourite restaurant in Tavira. The streets were fairly empty; I pretended we were on a movie set made especially for us. At night, the quaint streets were shrouded in a burnished yellow-orange glow from the lamps. The restaurant was packed and looked like somebody's bathroom without a tub. The walls were covered with blue and white plant-patterned tiles. Why do the Portuguese like tiles so much?

The owner was on his own, an elderly, overwhelmed white-haired man in his sixties, rushing around attempting to serve everybody on time. We waited about an hour for our meal. In that time we kept ourselves busy. Alice liked to be entertained. If not there was hell to pay, followed by a huge strop or tantrum.

"Let's play hangman!

"Let's play parson's parcel.

"I know a game…

"I'm bored, Daddy, I'm bored!"

Alice let slip embarrassing revelations about Balthazar and some of his exes while he sat there, flushed and uncomfortable. Apparently Balthazar had had so many different types of girlfriends, he referred to them by country.

Eventually our meal of cataplana arrived, a seafood stew served with rice and chips. It was delicious. I hate wine but gulped it down as though it was water.

Upon our return to the apartment, Alice went to bed and, slightly tipsy, I grilled Balthazar. "So how long have you been fucking Tara behind my back?"

He shifted in his seat, sipped from his glass of rum.

"About a month," he said.

"That weekend at Brigette's house when we were ironing out our issues, you'd slept with her before coming down." My voice was calm but it sounded like a stranger's, as though somebody else would walk into the room wanting to claim it.

"Yes." He held my gaze. I was reminded of a bug trapped under a glass, how it must feel both horror and wonder stuck in that tall object. The distance between "no" and "yes" is a gulf, with the ability to change outcomes.

I slowly blew out a soundless breath wanting to blind him with invisible smoke from my mouth.

"If you like sleeping with her so much why don't you have a relationship and stop wasting my time?"

He placed his hand on my thigh. "God you're pretty," he murmured. "and unusual."

I swatted his hand off. "Stop trying to touch me, you're not entitled anymore."

He looked annoyed, moving restlessly. "I admit," he began tentatively, "there is a sexual connection between Tara and I but not in any other way. She's reckless and wild but…"

"Oh bullshit, Balthazar, she's exactly the kind of woman you like. All that nomad shit, it must be great for your ego to have a grown woman acting crazy over you, climbing through windows to get to you." I took a sip from my glass of rum, letting the sweetness wash over my tongue.

"Firstly, I don't have a type. You and I have much more of a bond in different ways. I really fancy you but I knew I could have her whenever I wanted. I don't feel the same way about her. Her bizarre behaviour doesn't impress me. It doesn't prove love. It just shows she's nuts," he said, pinning me with an earnest look, managing to seem sincere and regretful.

"It didn't stop you though, did it?" I said, slamming my empty glass on the table and then pulling it back as if ready to take aim. He winced, looking defeated.

Our duel continued for about two hours, knowing how intellectually dexterous Balthazar was—he could run rings around people in an argument in the most laid back, non-aggressive way—seeing him swallow my disdain was comforting. Taking chunks out of him was the most fun I'd had since arriving in Portugal. Eventually, he slinked off to the bedroom.

Later I joined him, slipping into the opposite end of the bed; the space between us was enough to accommodate all our belongings. At one point on his return from the toilet, he stood in the doorway studying me. We watched each other warily. Bathed in that deceptive lamplight, groggy, I thought he was covered in pulsing, bloodied hearts. Then the hearts were morphing into another man, a Balthazar I didn't know standing beside him. I couldn't tell if the blood was his or mine. I wanted to ask him, looking at the uncooked meat covering his body, "Are you going to eat that?"

It rained the following morning so we couldn't have breakfast on the terrace. Instead, we sat in the kitchen eating croissants with strawberry jam and thick cold cuts of salami in white buns that threatened to spill more secrets as though they were tongues. Balthazar was unusually less chatty, studying me discreetly whilst attempting to control Alice. Instead of eating, her head was bent over a piece of paper she was filling with abstract shapes and squiggles.

In the privacy of the bedroom, I confronted him. "You're fairly subdued this morning," I said on my feet, eyeing Balthazar who lay on the bed in a green and black checked shirt.

"I've been thinking a lot, darling," he said, "and it's just not working out for me. Since you've come I've felt deflated, depressed and subdued. Your being here has completely changed the dynamic between Alice and me, she's behaving differently."

I rocked back on my heels, steadied myself. "I've travelled for hours to get here, Balthazar. What exactly are you saying?"

He sat up, running a hand through his hair. "Look, you were in trouble and out of the kindness of my heart I offered to help but this is a special time for me and Alice. This isn't a holiday for you to bond with her!"

"I thought you'd be happy we were getting on. This is bullshit," I roared.

He swung his legs over the bed and stood up. "No! I have a right to express how I feel. It's my holiday with my daughter and I very kindly offered to share it with you. I'm sorry you like my children more than you like me but frankly, you wouldn't have that connection with them if not for me."

"Oh, so you're throwing me out! Thanks for coming to the rescue, asshole. I can't believe this." I stormed around, circling him.

"I'm not throwing you out. Why are you so stubborn? Listen to what I'm saying. Either we try to get along or I'm happy to pay for you to go back to Lisbon. You could stay here in Tavira but rent a room elsewhere; it's just some options. You've been cold to me since you arrived, very prickly. You won't let me touch you. I thought you came with forgiveness in your heart." His face was flushed, he paced back and forth.

"It's been three days!" I spat. "What do you expect? I have a right to be angry, I'm not going to put that aside so you're comfortable, no way. It's not as if I've treated Alice any differently just because I can't stand you right now."

"That's exactly it." His eyes narrowed. "Your behaviour is affecting her. I feel ganged up on and it's feeding into my relationship with her. You could use my daughter against me," he accused, throwing me a furious look.

"You're being an asshole, fine. I'll be out of your hair soon, as if this fucking trip could get any worse."

How dare he try to out-victim me!

"Darling, I'm just trying to resolve the situation," he whined.

I ignored him and grabbed my book, Banana Yoshimoto's *Kitchen*. I stomped off into the tiny veranda off the bedroom. I sat in the chair watching the road swell with cars and people, kicking myself. What does quiet fury sound like? Balthazar walked in, rested his forehead against mine. I decided that for however long I was in his presence I'd be polite, agreeable, to make him look even more of a bastard. I knew I would stay in Tavira, it would gnaw away at Balthazar knowing I was in the same town he loved so much. We agreed I'd return in the evening to pick up my stuff.

After they left, I sprang into action as though someone had slipped two Duracell batteries inside my back, slippers clicking on hot pavements. It didn't take long to find another residencial on the opposite side of the bridge. The door to the reception area chimed, the owner had a warm welcoming smile and a face that could have been made from dough. He told me he liked Sade and the room was light, spacious, balancing on the murmurs of the building.

Later, I walked the streets of Tavira. I sat on the bench next to an ice cream stand and watched the ripples of the river, wandering if loneliness could fill spaces. By evening, I returned to Balthazar's to pick up my bag. I hugged Alice and said goodbye, Balthazar's gaze a warm touch on my back. He offered me a lift, I refused.

In the morning, I sent him a text saying I wished he was on his own so I could shove him off one of the bridges. His response came quickly: *I thought you would understand. OK, then it's a wrap. Our chemistry is a perfect reflection of our complete lack of ability to see each other's point of view, shame. Maybe that's what sex does, allows us to live on the same planet without throwing each other off bridges. Charming. x*

An image of him drowning in a dark sea flashed in my mind but I knew that bastard probably swam out of the womb, so death by drowning was unlikely. Ridiculously charming, resourceful and incredibly well-travelled, he had an uncanny ability to survive most situations.

I turned down his offer for dinner and day trips two days in a row. By the third day, I was bored of my own company and walking everywhere. We called a temporary truce and decided to get along for the rest of our time in Portugal. We went bodyboarding at the beach, discovered an abandoned town on a boat trip to the border of Spain and ate greasy potatoes and chicken served by a pimply teenager at a beach restaurant. The volcanic ash disaster arrived just to make my holiday more uneventful, delivered by newsreaders in feverish tones. All over Europe it rendered people on holiday stranded, airports bursting with droves of erratic, flummoxed folk. We decided to keep moving, a band of three. On the overnight coach ride to Seville from Faro, we rode an endless tunnel, approaching a destination that may have shape-shifted by the time we arrived. Balthazar said, "I love you." I laughed it off.

In Seville it rained all day so we visited a gallery filled with Renaissance art. Balthazar was in his element, giving a breakdown of the artists and contexts to us. For dinner, we ate at a restaurant that looked like the inside of a giant wine barrel. There were huge slabs of smoked meat hanging from hooks in the visible kitchen. I forced myself to swallow some wine while Balthazar pacified Alice's mum on the phone. By all accounts, she believed he had somehow orchestrated the volcanic ash disaster to stop her daughter returning home to her. I smiled at this.

We caught a train to Madrid and in Madrid we caught another one to Barcelona. We were exhausted and tempers flared but Barcelona was unforgettable, vivid and vibrant. I bought Alice a straw hat which she placed on Bear Bear's head because he was getting heatstroke. An artist drew a caricature of all three of us; I slipped it into my bag imagining our sketched mouths feeding on bits of sunlight. Balthazar surprised me by borrowing a musician's harmonica and serenading me on the steps of Park Güell with his rendition of Little Walter's "Key to the Highway".

From Barcelona we took a train to Port Bou. During the journey, Balthazar charmed a family sitting across from us on the other side. I watched him swap contact details; I fished out a book to lose myself in. He had arranged to pick up a car in Port Bou where we would drive to Lagrasse and stay with a friend of his. We still had no idea when we'd get home.

We bolted out of Port Bou station, rumpled, crusty-eyed, slightly different versions of ourselves than we had been that morning. We didn't see the small changes happening but they caught up, winding us unexpectedly. Somewhere molecules had shifted.

Walking towards the blue Peugeot on that steep road, I realised I knew less about falling in love than I ever did and even less about knowing how to stay in love. And that honestly, I wasn't entirely blameless in all this. I'd been treating Balthazar as if he were the least significant thing in my life for months. It never occurred to me he would go elsewhere for comfort. Was I bad at letting people in? How do we reconcile between who we actually are and who our lovers imagine us to be? It was the possibility of knowing that drew us, that heady, seductive part of the process that made you look at the world through different eyes.

Bone tired from constantly travelling, we piled into the car. The Balthazar made of bloody hearts was driving us to Lagrasse, he said. The Balthazar I knew gave him directions. The sea below shimmered. The steep winding road was a glimmering nerve suspended between vast blue sky and all-encompassing earth. The shrinking landscape became smaller in the side mirror, blown away by exhaust pipe breaths. Alice began to talk like a chipmunk. Balthazar and I started arguing about the jacket he'd left on the train with his and Alice's passports inside, missing the lorry coming round a corner.

He swerved but too late, too far out. My stomach clenched, the car shuddered. Alice screamed. Then we were tumbling, hurtling into the mountains at full speed. And there were no hands at the wheel. Balthazar fell upon Balthazar, growling.

Fractures

Michael had to keep going back to the café La Cabane de Lumière—a glass panelled hub of delicious indulgence nestled under a golden arched doorway.

He made his way through the heaving streets of central London driven by his sweet tooth and a longing he felt growing inside. On Regent Street, the gold lettering etched on the building's sign glowed seductively. He imagined the structure leaking syrup and edible crème glues. The glass window displayed rum soaked rectangular delights and pot-bellied custard tarts dusted lightly with cinnamon. There were cakes in all sorts of guises; as ghosts, ships, cars, pumpkins and Wonder Woman, reminding him of an anecdote he'd heard. An artist's party had been thrown in the café. The artist arranged for a huge wedding cake, which took up the entire front section of the room. He arrived stark naked and proceeded to sit on the enormous confection, wallowing in the crumbling softness, feeling the intensity of gazes watching colours running on his pale skin and then serving fat globs of cake to the stunned guests. They'd swallowed, clapped and smiled thinly, all in the name of art.

It wasn't just the food that drew him there. After the door swished shut behind him and the scent of vanilla tickled his nostrils, he spotted her standing beside the counter chatting and laughing with another member of staff, a red-headed girl wearing a waistcoat over her shirt. Grace, his crush, was a young statuesque black woman with skin the colour of cocoa beans. Braided hair loosely tied back revealed a slim, angular face, dark brown eyes and a wide mouth.

Hair a little damp from his brisk walk and brandishing a tattered copy of *The Guardian* tucked under his arm, he headed for a corner booth. Its seats were still warm from previous occupants. The café's interior boasted a high white ceiling trimmed with gold, ornate hanging crystal chandeliers and white pillars. There were plush Burgundy leather chairs and black, circular tables. Large windows provided views of passers by ambling past. Menus in cranberry leather covers dotted the tables.

He'd walked in craving a tiramisu. Grace wandered over, her blue pen poised above a small pad.

"What will you have, sir?" She smiled distantly, politely. He flushed at the thought of wanting to know her intimately.

He saw himself through her eyes then: Filipino American male, six foot, handsome but probably not her type. He looked as if he'd slept in his wrinkled pinstriped suit and the stubble on his jaw itched. That undetectable gene that made him want to say inappropriate things kicked in.

Why do you look sad sometimes even when you laugh?

What are you most scared of?

Have you ever listened to Coltrane's "A Love Supreme"?

I don't have the language to say what it means; maybe you can interpret it better?

He said these thoughts internally, lifted his head abruptly as though she could hear them.

"Sir?" she enquired.

"Oh!" he replied. "I'd like scrambled eggs, two bagels, one hot chocolate and a piece of New York vanilla cheesecake."

She scribbled quickly, flashing another meaningless smile.

"Coming up!" She slipped the pad in her apron pocket

before darting off.

He watched her discreetly between mouthfuls; flitting from tables, realising her total disinterest wasn't personal to him. She wasn't warm, but efficient. She had a quiet confidence, an air about her that made you want to know more.

Sometimes he imagined her in his life, playing scenes in his head. In one, he was at dinner with his family, Grace by his side. His father attempted to make humorous conversation to lighten the atmosphere but failed woefully since his jokes were terrible. His mother's head sat practically buried in a deep bowl of Miso soup, snorkeling for her disbelief. His older brother eyed him resentfully. *Haha*, he thought, *not the centre of attention this time, shithead.*

His sister smiled admiringly, winking at him conspiratorially before the curtain of her sharp bob obscured the left side of her face.

At night he dreamt of lover's limbs entangled; twisting and turning always back to each other, to a centre. He tasted brown skin slick with sweat. He suckled Grace until she howled, burying his head in the valley between her breasts that felt knowable and caught fractures of light. He dreamt of aggressive sex, of hands around her neck squeezing while his body trembled its release. And smacks from a mean, metal-toothed belt buckling against her skin, wrenching far flung screams from her as though she were another country.

*

The café had its own symphony. In moments of stillness, Grace allowed it to wash over her. The jangling cutlery from the kitchen at the back, hissing kettles, cappuccino machines interrupting conversations, the door groaning as customers streamed in, a hum you could hear from outside. It was during such a moment the note arrived, delivered by manager Francois, a squat man with jowls and a permanently clammy forehead. He slapped it in her palm.

"For you!" he told her dramatically, wiping his hands on black trousers. "I see this is your personal residence now." His expression morphed into a fake scowl.

"Thanks, Francois. Nobody delivers things like you do." She ripped open the crème coloured envelope with a blood red seal.

A white card folded in two fell out. On the front was a sketch of her wearing a detached expression so uncannily accurate she laughed. She was holding a small treasure box with light bulbs spilling out of it. The note said:

For Grace, who dares to go hunting, a short poem to make you smile randomly throughout the day.
I listen for your heartbeat in the flurry of pigeons wings.
Your laugh fills a drained coffee cup,
The sadness in you will make a skeleton we can take to water,
Stars duplicate your jaw line and yell to street lamps,
They respond with light.

Say yes. One ticket reserved in your name to see Kurusawa's Rashomon, *this Saturday 8pm at The Ritzy cinema.*
Mxx
PS: Don't worry, I won't chop your body up into little pieces and shove you in a bin bag, at least not with a roomful of people around. ;-)

Whoever he was, his handwriting was beautiful, assured. It was slanted as though leaning against a storm. His words echoed inside as she served Chai teas, coconut truffles, bread and butter puddings. She was curious, excited. In this city that often created jaded versions of its inhabitants, how often did you truly receive a romantic, mysterious gesture? She was more intrigued than worried, happy to at least have this one thing to herself.

By lunch time the café was full. Grace scanned the faces of male customers, waiting for one to reveal himself as her admirer. There was the guy who always wore a grimy tweed jacket and only ever showed one hand. His left hand was hidden in his jacket sleeve. She guessed it was gnarled or a claw. Either way he was too busy scooping up mushroom soup with broken pieces of baguette to pay her any attention. A father whose frustrated expression screamed *I didn't sign up for this* admonished his kid through gritted teeth and threw embarrassed glances around. There was the old man at the back who sat starring at his croque monsieur. He was so still he had the aura of a stuffed animal. She ambled over.

"Excuse me, sir, do you want me to order something else for you?"

"I used to be a spy you know," he said distantly.

"Sure." She smiled patiently and signaled at Alberto and the other two waiters to keep watch. Midway through his tale of cold war days, Grace drifted.

What if Mxx had just been released from prison? What if he was a psychopath with a penchant for stalking unsuspecting women before sending them poetry? A man with an egg timer ran through her mind. The egg timer exploded and the man was left with no head.

Grace searched for the flat keys in her pocket, a little distracted by the sound of kids riding their bikes and squealing in the courtyard. Their voices mingled with car tyres screeching to a halt, traffic in the distance, the rumble of girls in the small playground out back, passing their future selves on each apparatus making noises they didn't understand. Grace shoved the key into the lock, saying a short prayer silently. She sighed, already bracing herself for that feeling of dread that would lodge in her throat. One of these days, she fully expected to see her twin sister Hilly on the other side, clawing at their childhood carcasses until there was nothing left.

She walked in, shutting the door carefully. She flicked the hallway light on, hanging her coat on the rack she'd almost smashed a finger nailing to the orange wall. The flat smelled of curry. Hilly must have cooked. She didn't bother calling out but she bumped into Hilly, whose lean, tall frame nearly knocked the wind out of her, whose face floated in the dark. Her onyx eyes bore into Grace's with barely concealed irritation.

"Oh, you're back," Hilly muttered, already turning away as though Grace being home was inconsequential. Grace dropped her rucksack by the white shoe rack. The clock read 11pm. *One day*, she thought, *one day Hilly might forgive me.*

Once, she'd dreamt about them in a gladiator ring, pitted against each other. The audience was made up of thousands of versions of their father, all sporting the same black whistle round their necks, the same caterpillar-like small scar on the corner of their lips, all trying to still a certain rage in their shoulders, cracking their left hand fingers intermittently. Grace's weapon had been a blood stained rounder's bat she and Hilly had found in the trunk of their father Odun's car aged ten, rolling over a pair of brown gloves, an ignition choking and the outline of the mouth it had silenced. Hilly's weapon had been Odun's worn leather belt, which she'd flogged Grace with relentlessly, winning the fight, the approval of their fathers cheering in the stalls, until she broke Grace's skin, resurrecting old injuries to the surface to mutate.

They were identical physically but different in many ways. When they were girls, Grace had been the outgoing, bubbly one, curious about everything. Hilly was surlier, insular, brooding. Grace liked Wonder Woman, comic books, carnival, Inspector Gadget, sour Coca-Cola bottle sweets and challenging the boys in their neighborhood to games of football she attached to bets where she'd managed to fleece a few out of pocket money and even a game boy.

Hilly preferred girly girls and occasionally following Odun on his runs, sitting in his beat up Green Vauxhall Cavalier, flicking the radio stations over and humming along to tunes she liked. Sometimes, she played with Elvira, the daughter of their babysitter. They painted each other's faces, braided their hair unsuccessfully, or played hide and seek indoors with the TV on full blast. As if either of them would attempt to hide in the scenes on the screen, bourbon sweet wrappers crinkling and whispering like second tongues.

Odun was a physically striking man. You couldn't help looking if you spotted him swaggering by. At 6 foot 3 he was intimidating, broad shouldered and ruggedly handsome. The son of a Trinidadian lawyer and a Nigerian nurse, he'd grown up in Trinidad. His skin was the colour of molasses and that sweet Trinidadian accent which made panties explode had a deceptively laidback charm that masked a steeliness and a dark temper. Odun delighted in playing his girls off against each other.

"Why can't you solve this equation?" he'd bark at Grace, checking over her math's homework book in the evening. "Hilly would have done this in two minutes! Do you want to be the stupid twin?"

Grace would shake her head, confused by the thunderous expression on his face, his looming figure leaning towards her and into her brain. Sometimes when they played in the park, he'd force the girls to race each other. Inevitably, being the slower of the two, Hilly would lag behind. And Odun would blow that damn whistle he wore, yelling, "Come on, catch her rass! You want to be the weaker twin? Are you my daughters or are you my daughters?"

"Yes sir!" they would answer, out of breath but pushing, limbs aching, arms pumping towards some invisible demon Odun had placed on the fading white line, growing in stature as the girls approached. And when they crossed the line, collapsing in a heap, Odun was waiting, scooping them up and raining kisses on their foreheads. "Milkshakes for my beauties! But Goddamit, Hilly, your timing needs to get better. You want to be Daddy's wingman one day or not?"

Now and again, the girls heard Odun throwing things in his room at night, before crying softly. They wondered whether it was their fault, whether he'd ever get over their mother Pearl dying giving birth, leaving him holding two girls who looked exactly like her.

Grace walked into the kitchen, sweeping the beading in the doorway to the side. It was too late to eat. She took a bottle of apple juice from the fridge, poured herself a glass while Hilly watched, leaning against the washing machine, holding her long, red false fingernails up, blowing on them.

"You see Odun today?" Grace asked, trying to keep her tone measured, light.

Hilly placed her hands on her hips, glaring. "Why do I have to be the one to go see that bastard? Why can't you do it after work or something? You think you're the only one with a life?"

"Because we're supposed to take it in turns remember? You haven't been the last three times. You know I can't go after work, visiting hours stop way earlier. Please? He's been asking about you. Hilly, he's dying," Grace muttered, rubbing her shoulders, watching the magnets on the fridge; little Tasmanian devils mid-motion as if they were running from the cold, from wounds the girls couldn't bring themselves to face.

"So big man Odun is dying and the world has to stop?" Hilly spat, grabbing a tangerine from the fruit bowl and peeling it swiftly. There were cigarette stubs in an ashtray on the counter, a rolling pin with bits of dough in the sink.

"Hilly, it's time." Grace stood, moving towards her sister to hold her, to give some sort of comfort.

"You know what? I wish he'd hurry up and die already." Hilly said, storming past, dropping a few orange coloured missiles in her wake.

It was summer when it happened. The girls were ten. It was so hot that Friday, they spent half their pocket money buying ice lollies and when those ran out, drinking from big Evian bottles they'd filled with a mixture of juices.

In the evening, Odun went out on one of his runs. The girls kept the big living room window open, watching soaps after a dinner of spaghetti and meatballs they'd cooked themselves. Grace would always remember small things about that night, shrinking and looming in the lens time built. She remembered the sound of the front door opening, thinking maybe Odun had forgotten something and come back, Hilly leaning her head against her shoulders on the aquamarine coloured sofa, the TV blaring loudly, an old episode of *Beadle's About* on.

A strange man appeared in the doorway and dragged away a screaming Hilly. Grace grabbed Hilly's hand as the man placed a finger over his mouth. She began to shake, she thought she'd faint but she held onto Hilly tightly as the audience's laughter on *Beadle's About* rose. Grace would always remember the sheen on the man's neck, his stocky build, his cheap smelling deodorant mingled with sweat, his pink tongue darting out over the maroon mask he wore that oddly made him look like a superhero. She'd remember her and Hilly being dragged into a blue car, the man's scarred hands at the wheel, the soft purr of the vehicle pulling away, a rolled up copy of *The Times* on the floor. And suddenly thinking she was older than Hilly by four minutes. Four minutes was a long time, anything could happen in four minutes! A 4 by 100 metres relay team could set a world record; a tree could fall and kill someone during a storm, at least three fireworks could be released into the night sky. What if Hilly had been born first? Maybe Pearl would have lived, maybe they wouldn't have been left to fend for themselves in the evenings because Odun had to bring money in. Maybe the man with the scarred hands would have kept away.

When they got to the house, they were locked in a room that had two dog bowls on the floor, a chintz curtain, a rabbit chew toy and a gun target silhouette pinned up near the window covered in holes. The dog kept barking in the garden. Grace thought she could hear its heart beating. It kept circling, getting closer. Then Hilly started crying and the man punched Grace repeatedly in the face, till the dog's heartbeat stopped beating in her chest, and its mouth travelled into the room, snapping at the last bits of light she saw. When she came round, Hilly was trembling in the corner, unable to meet her eyes, a damp, sticky patch on the front of her jeans shorts, drying into the shape of a small spaceship.

Odun rescued his girls two nights later. In the back of her mind, face aching, worrying that even worse was to come, Grace had always thought he would. When he burst through the door of that room after breaking it open, there were at least ten men behind him. He shook with anger, with relief, clutching his girls, desperately clinging to them for several minutes as if he couldn't believe they were real. On the way back home, Hilly was silent in the car.

Afterwards, the rumour was that Odun had set Michael Hayes alight, the man responsible for those terrible few days of that summer. Acting on behalf of his loan shark boss whom Odun owed a substantial amount of money, he'd kidnapped the girls in retaliation. Nobody ever found his body. Odun believed in the act of revenge, swift and uncompromising. He had one rule he swore by, you never touched a man's children. Ever.

Grace would never forget the night they came home. Odun sat in front of that large sitting room window in his white vest, legs up, smoking the biggest spliff she'd ever seen, daring anybody to come for his girls again, turning the whistle on his neck sporadically. He sat there for hours, refusing to let the girls out of his sight, smoking into the bloody edge of the night, where a gun target, a chew toy and a dog riddled with bullet holes met on ground made of old newspapers, arguing over who was the best witness before dying in their corners.

Grace knew Hilly would never forgive her. The girls struggled with nightmares for months afterwards. Sometimes, Grace would see the stain from Hilly's shorts that night in the corner of her nightmares, a tiny hovercraft edging its way over the dark, sometimes Hilly would appear, choking on the hovercraft before being rendered silent.

Grace decided not to press Hilly further. She was exhausted and didn't have the strength to argue. Instead, she soaked in the bath, listening to Nina Simone blaring from Hilly's room. Afterwards, standing naked in the mirror, she watched their organs float. She reached for Hilly's heart bleeding over her rib, trying to hold the beat, crying a little, murmuring apologies as the steam continued to fade.

In the morning, she woke to find Hilly standing over her, breathing heavily. She turned a photograph of Odun in her hands as though it were a weapon, then held it up to the light, scanning it searchingly, as if she'd left some belongings there.

Saturday rolled in. Grace told herself she wasn't going to go on the date set by the stranger. A lie she said out loud so her own words could hold her accountable. But she knew she was deceiving herself when she wore her lucky multi-coloured polka dot shirt teamed with ripped blue jeans and black ballet style flats. Hilly walked in on her checking her outfit in the mirror, eyed her suspiciously.

"Who's the guy?" she asked, grabbing a black cat suit she'd loaned Grace some weeks back, then handing Grace a deep raspberry hued lipstick from the dresser. "Here. Use this one. It's vampy."

"Just a friend," Grace said offhandedly.

"Some friend. You're wearing your favourite shirt. Odun would approve. He always liked your style. He loves you more you know. He thinks you're stronger," Hilly replied, tucking a stray braid back from Grace's forehead almost tenderly.

Grace caught the Central and Victoria lines, avoided eye contact with people in carriages and emerged from the station with a sigh of trepidation. She loved The Ritzy's organic feel and the screenings written on blackboards.

In the screening room there were only a handful of people. She sat right at the back to observe everybody else and keep watch on the entrance discreetly. A velvet red seat swallowed her bottom. *This is dangerous*, she thought. *I feel alive.* She adjusted her buttocks, some popcorn spilled, leaving a trail of small white clouds on her thighs. Soon, she was swept up in adverts; a silly mobile ad with a man running around a beach desperately trying to get a signal and a trailer for a terrible-looking medieval movie.

She felt his presence before seeing him. Her neck was warm, something danced on her skin. He stood to her left, light from the outlines on the screen played over his frame, as though he had somehow emerged from that same screen while the adverts were rolling, while she'd momentarily looked away. His movements were languid, confident. Dressed in worn black jeans, a retro yellow Bruce Lee T-shirt and a pair of battered green converses, he looked casual and relaxed. He sat next to her. Wearing a sheepish expression, he stirred his cookies and cream flavoured Ben and Jerry's ice cream.

She recognised him. He was the cute Asian guy who'd been coming to the café for roughly a month. He had an American accent she couldn't quite place, loved bagels and seemed to mull over problems that needed unpicking while he ate. There was a tiny, endearing gap between his two front teeth. Deceptively sleepy, slightly slanted eyes with long lashes crinkled at the corners as he smiled warmly. His hair was cropped close. From his darker skin tone she guessed he was maybe Filipino, Malaysian or Cambodian. He leaned over. "You must be a little crazy," he whispered. "Coming out to meet a stranger. My kind of woman. I'm Michael." He brushed a kiss the weight of a butterfly on her cheek.

"You smell nice," he added. "What is that?"

She choked back a laugh. "I'm Grace, but you already know that. You mean I don't smell like omelets and sausages for a change?"

"I have to admit, you wear the scent of omelets and sausages very well and you look good doing so."

They both laughed.

Grace slid some popcorn into her mouth. "You can share this with me," she offered, setting it back between her thighs.

Michael took off his jacket; a mobile phone went off. "Oh I'm counting on it, between getting our tickets and buying this shit, I'm actually broke. It's outrageous the charges for confectionary in cinemas. Don't worry; I can still buy you drinks."

She chuckled, leaning forward in her seat, holding his unwavering gaze with a probing one of her own. "Your poetry is odd," she said finally.

"You came," he answered, unable to stop a small grin, his opening of skin for her to sink her fingers into. He stretched his long legs, sank further back into the seat and wolfed down a couple more spoonfuls of ice cream.

"Are you familiar with Kurosawa?" he asked.

"I only saw one film of his," she answered honestly. "I saw *Seven Samurai* late at night on Film Four."

"The first time I saw you, you were serving this table of asshole City-types breakfast. They were rude. You seemed like you were ready to kick someone's ass. And I thought, there's a woman who looks like she has some spirit, some adventure in her," he said before turning back to the screen.

Afterwards, they sat in the bar area talking and listening to isolated sounds; glasses clinking, rims crawling off the short bar, a few orders trapped between the till opening and closing, drunken silhouettes scraping back against the shadows. She sipped glasses of Tia Maria, vodka and orange. He drank Jack Daniels mixed with coke, a brand of German beer she couldn't pronounce properly. Her body became sweaty, a result of her nerves and excitement. She found herself struggling to grapple with her feelings. He watched her through eyes that seemed to have tricks up their lids.

"What do you do?" she asked.

"I travel, write among other things. You like literature?"

"Yeah. James Baldwin, Dosteovsky, Zora Neale Hurston. Why the note? Why not ask me out in person?"

"Too easy. I wanted to intrigue you, plus the probability you might not show prolonged the anxiety. A man should wrestle with some anxiety if he likes a woman, don't you think?" he replied.

"You're a peculiar egg."

Michael kissed her, sucked her tongue. The kiss became heady. He tasted of alcoholic possibilities; of things in the dark she'd drawn with her fingers that needed faces and permission to quench their thirsts. Her fingers sunk further into his opening of skin.

"Say you'll see me again," he begged.

"Why?"

"Because I want to know the strange things about you."

Three weeks passed. On the evening Grace received the phone call from the hospital, she was standing by the dresser in her room. After she hung up, the phone fell from her hand. She needed to find Hilly. The pain in her head was so strong, as though someone had plunged a hot poker in there, tracing half signs in her brain she wouldn't be able to interpret till later, flashing in a darkness that was spreading. She tried to grab the signs but they remained illusive, flickering then thinning. She thought her head would explode.

She opened the packet of Codydramol on the dresser, swallowed two before collapsing on the bed. The ceiling spun. Tears ran down her cheeks as she reached for the photograph on the chest of drawers beside the bed, the one Hilly had been fascinated with for weeks. In it was a young Odun, handsome and smiling at the camera in his long black leather jacket, an afro comb tucked into his hair.

He seemed to be launching himself at the lens in a way that said, "World I'm coming, get ready for me." Just behind him on the steps of a house was the figure of a woman in a yellow dress, pregnant and looking at Odun with such an expression of love, it was almost palpable. She recognised those steps. A feeling of sickness rose through her throat. Pearl had lived in that house too, the home they grew up in. Odun had gotten rid of every scrap of evidence, every sign of her but somehow this photograph had resurfaced and who knew how long Hilly had been carrying it around. The resemblance between the girls and their mother was so uncanny; it could have been either Grace or Hilly in the picture, taking turns to sit in the yellow dress to watch Odun transforming into the man he'd become.

Grace closed her eyes. She could hear the sound of the fridge groaning. She saw herself and Hilly running towards Odun, crossing the white line of the park, only this time Pearl was beside them, arms outstretched, feet covered in white paint, tongue floating in the dark cavern of her mouth. She was running too, pregnant with the blueprints of things that would happen, her stomach extending towards that line, her hands waving frantically. Grace climbed off the bed, ran into the bathroom retching in the toilet. Afterwards, she stumbled towards the front door, clutching her stomach, reaching for the handle. She walked into the night almost blindly, calling Hilly's name to the luminous signs from her head that had made their way into street corners.

"You look a little different tonight," Michael commented. "This updo suits you, you have an elegant neck."

Hilly smiled, noticing the few paintings of kimonoed women on the walls, the birdcage in the corner by the bar, the dark décor. She liked his choice of a moody, atmospheric discreet Dim Sum restaurant that served unusual cocktails with exotic ingredients. After reading their text message exchanges on her sister's phone, it had been a simple decision to come. Why should Grace have all the fun? It was easy enough to pretend to be Grace, she'd done it on and off secretly for years. She ordered spicy duck, he ordered some seaweed dumplings. She wondered if Grace had fucked him yet.

Later, they threaded their way through less busier streets. A puffy-eyed, bald-headed man attempted to sell them drugs opposite Brixton station. The air felt charged between them. They meandered over to the new water garden. An oasis of green, dotted with bright rings of flowers, ponds and small seating areas. It was empty, flanked by a few trees. He held her hand and they wandered in, towards a broad trunked Sycamore tree. Hilly didn't notice the tears running down the face of the female statue sitting cross-legged in a pond. Instead, her focus was on the oval shaped, large silver capsule beyond that area, burrowed in the grass with a bubbled glass window and dimmed yellow light emanating from it.

"It's that memory capsule that's been spotted around the city," she explained. "I think it's some sort of movable art installation. People write their favourite memories of London on cards or scraps of paper and slip it in."

"Come on," he said, tugging her forward. "Let's have an adventure."

He opened the capsule door easily and they entered. She barely spotted the white screen and gearstick when the lights went off. She could feel the scraps of paper beneath her feet.

All evening something had been gnawing at her, a terrible feeling of dread that had been growing which she'd ignored but couldn't any longer. The pain in her chest was searing. She couldn't breathe. Odun had died. She knew it; she felt that last breath leave him.

Michael wouldn't let her off. Instead he said, "I forgot to tell you: I'm not from anywhere you'd know."

He loomed towards her, his mouth widened, twisting and silver in the dark till she thought it would swallow her. The engine came on. The capsule hovered above the ground.

Oh God, Hilly thought. She felt something prick her skin. She counted to ten, her limbs slackened, she couldn't feel her body anymore. She tried to stop the panic rising. Grace would come because she owed her. Odun wasn't coming. He'd kicked the bucket. Goddamn him.

She fell to the floor crying on the city's memories, turning her head to the light in the window, desperately trying to stretch her hand out to trace the shape of a whistle rising through the bubbled glass.

Walk With Sleep

The bomb shelters resembled museums waiting for the flurry of movement. At each one—Camden Town, Belsize Park, Goodge Street, Chancery Lane, Stockwell, Clapham North—there was no exit for underground jumpers.

Brick ventilation shafts on the roofs of tunnels waited for them. At Clapham South, shelter doors whispered. The big lift was still in use. Haji and October rode it several times, watching expectantly as the door creaked open. They slid down the spiral staircase that burrowed into the tunnel. At the bottom, the walls bore directions for a canteen, shelter and medical areas. The empty control room was dusty with bits of wood in corners. They stroked the old board missing its emergency alarms. The bunks rolled out one after another, empty of bodies. It was like a forgotten town, ready for them to invent their own subterranean language. October discovered a broken safe storing abandoned government files, filled with documents on World War II. She pored over them. They wandered the rooms, running their hands over items.

Haji told her about his constant battle to feel at home in his own body while he'd been alive. He had never been diagnosed, never sought the advice of medical professionals but he'd always known something wasn't quite right. The random attacks of disconnection he experienced made him feel awkard around people. At social gatherings he found himself holding his breath, watching and waiting for the body parts he couldn't feel to appear at the opposite end of the room, his leg parting through the crowd towards him to claim ownership, his arm bruised from all the times it had attempted to lift Nuri off the ground after it was too late. Once at a gallery launch, he'd been so panicked that he had spilled his glass of white wine on the pristine white tablecloth, leaving a baffled group of people to rush into the toilet. There, he had felt his face in the mirror frantically, convinced it was made up from the parts of others. Haji had curled into a ball on the cubicle floor, wanting to flush his head down the toilet.

Sitting up on an empty bunk listening to him, October began to whimper softly.

"You've been here a long time haven't you? Years," she said, wiping her tears, trying to steady her rising shoulders and the panic in her voice.

He nodded gravely. "It's a funny place this world, there's no artifice. Somehow, I feel more of a sense of myself here without all the noise."

"But don't you feel lonely?" October asked, searching his face.

He laughed, running a finger over the space on his shirt a button had come off. "I felt lonelier out there, surrounded by all those people chasing ideas of happiness that weren't even theirs." The silence that followed felt thick, melancholic.

October was grateful Betty had dozed off. "I remembered something earlier," she said, stumbling over her words a little. "When I bought Betty, the lady at the shop who served me said, 'I still do that sometimes.' What do you think she meant?"

Haji did not answer but smiled patiently instead, watching her hands morph into small traps.

Before

On the morning of her audition October counted thirty women in the cold, narrow audition hallway, imagining wax figures of everybody melting on a conveyor belt that stopped each time a figure flattened. She sat wringing her hands nervously, every now and again looking at the white audition room door at the far end of the hallway. It swung open each time an actress walked out, creaking loudly in satisfaction. At the opposite end, the water machine chugged, dampening the sounds of heels clicking in the various rooms. Large headshots of famous, successful actors and actresses lined the walls. October watched each one take a bite from the same never-ending piece of cake before passing it on. Sated, the actors' bodies then leaned forward, threatening to leave their frames to wander the long hallway mockingly.

She'd gone to twenty-five different auditions in the last month and hadn't gotten one central role; only features as an extra in *Eastenders*, *Holby City* and *Coronation Street*. She was planning to try her luck with theatre instead to see how that panned out. She'd visited The Tricycle Theatre a few times, staring at their posters, drinking at the bar and waiting for the actors to emerge from their heady nights of performance.

She took a deep breath and the conveyor belt now surrounded her, the wax figures had disappeared but the actresses in various states of undress held items October recognised; a pair of torn period-stained tights, a pale parasite that had begun to grow tiny legs on her bedroom window sill at nights, her mother's gold ring she'd had to sell to help pay rent months back. She blinked the image away and the women were all back in their seats again, restless, adjusting their costumes, checking their reflections for silences in small make-up mirrors.

She took another deep breath, aware of every leg uncrossing, every panicked whisper, every body leaning towards an invisible, darkening line. She ran her lines over in her head to keep her calm.

When the heavyset woman with a severe bun and a clipboard called her name, October stood up steadily, sensing the eyes of the other actresses on her but not the faintest of smirks on some of their faces.

The audition room was a plain, underwhelming experience; white walls, a wooden floor, an open skylight. The producer and director of the drama—both men—and a surly-looking, chestnut haired, grey-eyed woman sat behind a table. They got brief pleasantries out of the way before indicating she should start.

October gave her interpretation of the scene she'd been sent; a pirate battling on the seas, his tormented love, a reckoning on an unnamed Caribbean island. Her audition lasted ten minutes. She searched their faces expectantly after her last line. They thanked her for coming, smiling politely, their expressions unreadable. Then the director stood and ushered her to one side. His lanky frame momentarily blocked her view of the others.

"You were very good," he offered flatly. "Erm... This is awkward. The part wasn't written for a black woman."

October pulled her arm back, the small embers of anger flickering. "It didn't say so in the casting call. I don't understand, some of it is set on a Caribbean island. Why couldn't I play a pirate's wife? You're the director. Doesn't your decision stand?" Her voice rose then. Behind the table, the producer and the woman, shifting awkwardly, looked everywhere but at her.

"I'm sorry, my hands are tied. I'm only telling you because I feel it's cruel not to. You really are very good and very attractive. Good luck," he said, face flushed, already turning his back.

She passed through Deptford market feeling angry and frustrated. From the Sense charity shop doorway, she spotted a Betty Boop T-shirt on a rack. It was the last one of the lot, rumpled a little from all the hands that had decided to pass on it. Stepping into the shop, she felt herself already reaching for it and the bitter wind whipping her items from the audition conveyor belt all around her.

*

Haji jumped after the thing inside him wouldn't stop growing. For years he fed it with samosas, curries, koshary, gin. At sixteen he stepped back from the mirror when his mouth looked unrecognisable, cruel, superimposed.

School meant trying to sit still in lessons pretending he didn't feel disconnected from his limbs. He took to carrying a wind-up man in his pocket which he'd place on the playground floor during breaks, starring at it in deep concentration, trying to find the centre of its movement as though it would reveal something. Girls would giggle at the edges, finger their pleated grey skirts and say, "Are you okay Haji? You're acting funny."

"Go away," he'd retort, barely glancing their way, listening for more important things such as a second heartbeat he was sure was winging its way to his lean, rangy frame.

"Why don't you disappear? You're a weirdo," the girls would snap, narrowing their eyes, reducing him to a tiny flint as they stomped off before breaking into fits of laughter again, coddled by the headiness of youth.

On Wednesday 26 February his life came crashing down, a broken mauve eggshell on the black and white kitchen floor. The photo of the boy he once was with a laughing woman rested on the counter top, the wooden frame still greasy from an incident during which he couldn't feel his arm; he'd been shelling prawns when that horrible, murky feeling came. He grabbed the photograph as though it was a lifeline.

It irked him that he had no memory of the photo, only that they were happy. He picked up his egg shell with trembling fingers, dumping the fragments in the detachable head of the blue bin, a purgatory for all the wind-up men that had accompanied him over the years. He brushed his teeth, downed a glass of orange juice. He didn't close the fridge door, shut the windows or check the plugs were turned off. The chipped purple door of flat 49b slammed shut.

Outside, the air was cold on his skin. The sky snatched facial expressions, swirling them grey. Haji observed the scenes around him; a man paying a bike messenger outside a tall, soulless office block, laughter between two charity fundraisers shaking their orange buckets at the traffic lights, a shop shutter door opening, its slow, mechanical sound reverberating in his ears.

At Bank station the platform was hot. People avoided each other's gazes. Their voices were locusts scratching his throat. The time was 11am. The clock had hands on its face, which made him laugh and wonder what it would be like to have fingers and limbs sprouting out of his face. The station was one cavernous passage, churning out passengers bearing faded bruises from 5am till 1am daily.

The feeling of sadness persisted, holding his body hostage. For ages he had felt nothing, had been numb. He had simply functioned. Now he thought about the tube train and how it ran through tunnels, heartbeats, chests, through guts that grew comets and tongues twinned the flame. The tube transported worlds intersecting. Oily spillage slipped through its programmed doors. The underground brought deliverance. The rumbling train approaching presented an exit. The sound of shutter doors trapped in his ears and the train wheels screeching seemed to be in collusion. To Haji, the driver was an angel in disguise who could change at any moment in his neat, private carriage.

Haji's right arm went dead first. He leapt in front of the train just as his left arm was about to, making the woman in the cream Mac jacket standing behind him gasp for breath. Everything and everyone shrunk, reduced to deflated things orbiting in the distance, the past. He landed inside the void, the thud of his fall splitting the driver's head, leaving miscellaneous anxieties there to torment him for months.

*

She stood punching the tunnel walls with its thick black cables, frustrated her fists weren't scraped raw. It was after 2am and the trains had stopped running. Mice scurried along the tracks in quick bursts. The glow of light from the platform made parallel worlds split. She stopped punching, fists by her side. She glanced at the walls, silently cursing. Haji wondered why she didn't pick up the crooked smiles that had slipped from passengers and were circling her feet. It was one of the beauties in this afterlife. The dark lay behind her, waiting to swallow. Haji ambled over, the soles of his shoes gone. The tracks had eaten them.

On closer inspection, the dark-skinned black woman with locks hanging down to her shoulders had a newbie's air about her with high cheekbones and a stubborn, full mouth. She wore a blue Betty Boop T-shirt. She turned to face him.

Betty moved too.

Betty sat in the blue, hand on jaw and frowned. "Let's see if this schmuck will be of any use," she said.

"Shut up, Betty!" The woman ordered. "Can you let me think?"

"Hey, you okay? I'm Haji." He stretched his hand out awkwardly, as though he'd borrowed someone else's arm and was adjusting. He always did that in close proximity of an attractive woman.

She ploughed her fingers through her locks, shoving them back. "Can you help me? We're lost. We've been trying to get out of the underground for days and just end up going from one station to the next. We can't seem to leave and it's driving me crazy. I'm October, this is my T-shirt Betty," she said.

"Um yeah, I know Betty Boop," he answered.

October leaned forward and whispered, "Listen, Betty's in between jobs right now. You know, with the whole economic climate thing? She's a little sensitive."

"Okay." Haji shot a cautious glance at her T-shirt. Betty was playing cat's cradle with the smiles; she paused momentarily to flutter her lashes at him. "I've been down here for a long time," Haji continued. "There are limitations to what I can do."

"But you can help us get out of here, right?" October asked.

"No, you jumped. There is no way out for jumpers into the real world."

"No, no, no, no, no! I'm lost. I keep trying to tell you people this but nobody down here seems to understand. I have a meeting to go to."

"I'm sorry, but you jumped, otherwise you wouldn't be here."

"Look," she said urgently, "I didn't have a reason to kill myself. I have no need to be here. Is there a way out of this place or not?"

Haji grimaced, his mouth thinned into a flat line. "Yeah, there is. It's an opening near the old bomb shelter. It will take us a while to get there, even then there's no guarantee we can get through."

October rubbed her head roughly, as if it was a scratch card with numbers underneath. "Can't you get us there any quicker? You must know all the shortcuts," she asked.

"Look," Haji said, his impatience rising to the surface. "I'll take you the way I know, okay?"

"Fine." October started marching ahead.

"Loser," Betty chimed.

"Where did you get the T-shirt?" he asked, rubbing his jaw.

"You mean Betty? Sense charity shop in Deptford. It was the last one on the rack," she answered nonchalantly.

Haji felt beads of sweat popping on his neck. His brown eyes moistened at the memory of his mother taking him T-shirt shopping, how opposite their tastes were. His latte-coloured skin looked pallid in the light.

"Also Betty asked me to," October remarked, running her tongue over her lip. "She said, 'Honey, can you get me out of here? The sound of that register is driving me insane'."

Haji laughed and Betty yawned. October stopped, turning to face him. "So why did you kill yourself?"

*

The city carried you like its infant child then bled you. It put the night in you, snacking on all the injured silhouettes you acquired. The city taught you how to build fortresses of sound you could never dismantle. It kept you falling till hitting the ground became the necessary act of an unnamed religion.

In the old life, when he talked to himself in his empty flat, he imagined his internal conversations were collected like shiny coins slotted in machines. When the loneliness got overwhelming, he'd sit in cafes just to listen, curling his hands into balls. He'd watch people come and go, wanting to fill their bags with things that had galloped inside him, grazing his organs to leave their mark. After his shadow had abandoned him, running off with the dawn, he started loitering in those cafes, sometimes unable to feel his left side, convinced that Nuri had lured it away from the city.

Years ago, that bleak afternoon, Mama took to the sitting room with a headache. She switched off the freezer so the ice fell in soft, melting chunks and unplugged a blender filled with tomatoes, chilies, onion and coriander. Were it not for the rain, they would have been outside in the garden, firing sticks at tin cans sitting like targets waiting to grow legs.

He and Nuri, aged twelve and thirteen were bored, play-fighting with two squash rackets through the house. They fought on the maroon carpeted stairs before Nuri dashed into the bathroom. He ran after her, waving the racket, playfully twisting his face into a menacing expression. He pushed the door open. Nuri slipped and smashed her head against the sink. It happened so quickly he barely caught his breath. The room stood still. Nuri didn't get up, her racket free from her grasp. He couldn't recall dropping his racket, although he must have done it. A feeling like pins and needles took over his arms. He wasn't able to move them. Her head was bleeding, the blood running into the stillness. He stumbled against the silver towel rack, noticing his old Action Man figurine on the window sill, Nuri's blue roller-skates in the tub, wheels coated in mud and his father's big white pants slung over the shower railing, waiting to fall like some deflated parachute. How he'd made it downstairs escaped him but he'd always be haunted by the slow horror that crept into his mother's gaunt face and coming back up to be with Nuri; her not moving, talking or breathing. He was hypnotised by the small Action Man beside her, blood running into its eyes, his mother screaming and him not being able to remember whether he'd moved the Action Man.

After they buried Nuri, his parents started arguing in Arabic constantly. For months his mother's face always twisted into an expression he couldn't get away from. Nuri's death had been an accident but his mother never recovered, abandoning them and moving back to Egypt. He was left with a father who chewed pine nuts relentlessly, barely spoke to him and looked at him as if he were nothing. So he stored his guilt in limbs that increasingly felt alien to him. Sometimes he'd sit in Nuri's room, punching the body that had let him down, holding her roller-skates, crying, trying to forget. But the memory of he and Nuri carrying atlases and hopping over low fences remained, as if they were holding worlds and crossing them simultaneously.

*

He told October about Nuri while watching the light dance in her hair. She tucked her arm through his as though it belonged there. "I'm sorry. You're never the same after a loss like that. Have you run into your sister since?"

He shook his head, drew her closer. "For a while, I kept expecting her to show and she'd be the same you know? The same age and have that recklessness about her I remember, coming at me at full speed in those blue roller-skates. It never happened and I can't go to her."

"Why not?"

"I told you, I'm trapped here."

They paused for a bit, looking up at the blackened ceilings as if a constellation of stars would crash through that they could give individual names and identities. Betty sat up sucking her thumb and blinking at them.

In a carriage, October folded her legs like a Buddha, her lips pursed. Haji wanted to taste and trace her most recent memories; he felt a yearning to be close to her. He missed the taste of Guinness, missed the sky at night. He missed watching mindless TV while the roots within him begged to be uprooted and eating kebabs late at night with girls who could be slotted into neat categories.

October levitated, floating towards him.

"Show-off," Betty muttered.

He wanted to tell October he didn't ever want her to leave. She was the one person that made him long for company since he'd been dead. He wrestled with the thought, as if somebody had dropped it inside him while he wasn't looking. He didn't know what to do with it.

October began to spin, whipping through the carriage.

"Stop it!" Betty whined. "You're making me dizzy."

October continued, gathering speed, light.

"I'm going to be sick!" Betty yelled.

October stopped, tugging down the T-shirt that had shot up, exposing her belly button. "I have my appointment in a few days."

"You still think that's happening?" Haji asked sarcastically.

October's face fell and Betty struggled for breath in the blue.

On the Central line they stood on top of trains and pretended to be airplanes taking off runways. The Northern line brought leaps off the heads of passengers. Inside a District line carriage Haji lay his head on a woman's chest listening to her heartbeat because he sometimes got nostalgic. He smiled when she touched that exact spot and the hairs on her arms stood like soldiers to attention.

They pressed their faces on the windows to make masks of glass that would fade instantly. They held onto coattails and skirts, laughed when the people tried to get through ticket machines with them in tow and the machines read *Seek Assistance*. All the noise was a black and frothing sea they swam in. They removed the company names and logos from adverts. They napped on escalators and Betty moaned throughout. Haji showed October how to steal shoelaces from passengers and make model parachutes using them.

Along the way they passed other ghosts he had helped, who would nod sombrely. Sometimes Haji introduced her to them, like Manny, the pimp, who had a penchant for wearing jumpsuits. A metallic jumpsuit had clung to him when he'd been shoved onto the tracks by a vengeful prostitute at King's Cross station. He'd been dressed for adventure, a couple of LSD pills inside him, but all that waited were black train tracks. There was Laurie Lee, the blonde American who ran around in her dirty wedding dress. She'd died on her wedding day having caught her groom fucking her best friend in the church toilet an hour before they were to say I do. Carried along by despair, shaky and disorientated, she'd slipped to her end at St Paul's station. And Bruiser, the thirteen-year-old boy who'd always wondered what it would be like to fly. One day at Oxford Circus station he'd thought he could. He'd flown to his death. Every time they bumped into him he asked, "Have you seen my rabbit?"

They all had stories to tell.

Four days of discovery passed for October. They swung off fat cables on the walls along the way, relishing how agile their bodies were. They sought refuge underneath the trains, catching sparks with keen tongues. They pilfered abandoned purses from platforms, pretending the items were theirs. They travelled neon silhouettes on fate's blueprint. The tunnels kept unfurling and breathing as the dark, fat veins of the city.

After

It was early morning, footsteps above echoed around the room. October flew at him. "Liar!" she yelled, pummelling his shoulders. "There is no way out of here. I've followed you to every one of these stupid shelters and you've led me on some wild chase for nothing. You said–"

"I wanted to get to know you, to spend time with you so I told you what you needed to hear. I don't feel bad about it, it's hard down here sometimes," he replied, wiping his hands on creased brown trousers, a result of their night spent in the shelter.

Betty stood, looking back and forth between them. Haji turned his back, stalking off towards the direction of the main station.

"That's right, walk away, don't finish what you started," October spat, following.

Haji paused, his face contorted as though some internal battle was happening. "You're meant to be here, that's why you are."

"What?" October replied. "That's not true." She shook her head, eyes watering.

"Get rid of that T-shirt," he demanded.

"No!" Betty yelled. "Don't listen to him. He's a liar." Her huge eyes were saucers of rage. October pulled the T-shirt against her body protectively.

Haji pointed his finger at her. "Stop doing that! I'm not

going to pretend anymore."

Betty covered her ears. "Don't trust him. Can't you see what he's doing?"

"The night you died, you didn't get that part, did you?" Haji asked.

The sound of a siren began to flood her head. One of the last sounds she'd heard that night. "I told you, I was celebrating, I got cast in this new show due to start filming in Manchester and it is a big part..." Her words petered off.

"And this appointment you've been singing about non-stop?" Haji said.

"A meeting with the directors. I need to find a way out, they'll be wondering what happened. They scouted me for it you know! That night on the platform, it was Betty who told me to jump. I had been drinking and I listened to her."

He grabbed her shoulders, shaking them. "Stop it! You jumped, Betty's not real. Stop pretending she is."

October crumpled to the floor. "You're jealous of Betty! You're just another person telling lies about her." She began to cry, tasting the cut on her lips from her leap all over again, remembering reaching for a light she thought she could mould in those seconds, a snapshot in the memory of passengers on the platform.

He held her while she sobbed against him, contemplating an afterlife of skylines in tunnels, the sound of trains and the desire to slip into the spaces between them. She thought of time spent haunting carriages, people who leave and take their nomadic tendencies along with them. She screamed.

By 6am Clapham Junction station was a hive of activity. On platform 1 lay a crumpled T-shirt on the floor beside a clear, plastic half-filled bin. It twitched. A man in a grey suit with a flapping purple tie bent over it, stretching his hand.

The cartoon figure of Betty Boop looked up at him, still in the blue.

Meanwhile, sporting only her bra and trousers, October ran beside Haji on the tracks towards the sound of an oncoming train, towards the spot on the platform she fell from to re-enact her death, because she had to, because Betty whispered she hadn't gotten it right.

As the days rolled on, Haji and October chased past injuries, eluding them under faint cracks of light. A slow releasing static sparked in their brains, new internal weather that made them delirious on some instances, despondent on others. Haji was her audience. Sometimes he held the outlines of items from his sister's death guiltily while October performed hers; the squash racket, his mute Action Man, one roller-skate wheel caked in mud spinning, blotting small versions of death. On those occasions, when October's fall coincided with him curling and uncurling on the tracks, they'd crawl into each other afterwards, remembering what it was like to be human. And Betty's mouth would hang open in the blue, misshapen from this routine.

Each time.

Why is Pepe Canary Yellow?

In the Ilford branch of Barclays Bank, Pepe, dressed in a yellow chicken costume, was laughing with a security guard over his outfit. Five minutes earlier, he'd walked in and pretty much everyone had cracked a smile. *Must be raising money for charity*, they thought. *But where's his bucket? Must be hot in that.* His arrival had changed the mundane routine of the bank. *What a good sport!* was a silent shared thought among all. The security guard wearing a name tag that read *Andy* patted him on the back and somewhat smugly said, "You're a braver man than me, not sure my wife would look at me the same way if I went out in that!"

Pepe threw his head back chortling, then suddenly pulled a gun from the pocket of his costume. He fired two shots in the opposite wall, putting a hole through a large banner that read, *We give you value for your money!* in the process. Realisation dawned in split seconds. People dived to the floor screaming. When the shots were fired, the security guard instinctively swayed to the left.

Keeping a firm grip on him, Pepe said, "This has been a very bad week, Andy. Nobody needs to get hurt, so don't be stupid. Anyone of you cogs in the wheel raises the alarm and I'll put a bullet in him." His voice was calm, the cadence musical, as if he was buying presents for his grandmother rather than robbing a bank.

The tension in the room was palpable. The sound of pens

rolling on the countertops was enough an accompaniment to the heavy breathing to jar stillborns crossing over to a separate horizon. The guard felt the warm trickle of piss down his left leg.

Pepe spotted a slender woman with scraggly, unkempt brown hair, shielding her baby in a pram. Her right arm twitched uncontrollably.

Pepe nudged the guard forward, gun pressed against his spine in an open-mouthed kiss. "Stay there, Andy, don't try anything clever," he ordered. "I just want to make it clear to everybody that I'm not going to hurt anyone. This is about banks fucking us over, not you. I'm one of you. I'm on your side, so please stay calm." He walked over to the woman, touching her trembling arm lightly. "Look at me," he ordered. "Nothing bad is going to happen to you or your baby, okay?"

The woman nodded slowly, taking a deep breath. Pepe noted the absence of a ring. "Sorry about the stress, love." He stroked the baby's bewildered face. "He's got your chin. You a single mother?"

The woman uncurled her body, took a slow breath. "Yeah, it's just j-j-just me and Roddy," she stammered.

"Salt of the earth, single mothers! My mum was one," Pepe said conversationally, throwing a warning look at the guard who stared open-mouthed, sweat rings in the armpit areas of his white shirt.

"She ran a breakfast club for mothers," Pepe continued. "You should join one or set one up. Who helps you with him?"

"My mother does now and again," The woman offered shakily. "But she's got a bad knee. I feel guilty leaving him with her sometimes."

Pepe chuckled. "Nah, I'm sure she loves being a grandmother, probably enjoys having the company! Bet you like visiting your grandmother, don't you, little man?" Pepe offered the baby his finger. The boy grabbed it, giving a toothy smile in return. His face lit up as he laughed.

"Haha! See?" Pepe said. "He's got this sussed. You're a little diamond, mate."

She smoothed down the boy's woolly blue top with a shaky hand. "I've heard of those breakfast clubs but…" She looked into Pepe's dark eyes. They were warm, twinkling. Something in them made her feel a sense of affinity, she couldn't explain it. "It's so hard lately, Roddy's the only thing that keeps me going. It's a good idea."

"Life will be a little easier. You'll make friends," Pepe assured her. "God, the women in my mother's club were great! Knitting maniacs, we were swimming in knitted items at my house. I even took it up at one point, very therapeutic! You'll be alright, love." Pepe squeezed her shoulder, smiling warmly. The people cowering on the floor watched their exchange wide-eyed, as if finding themselves in a play nobody had warned them they would be in. The four tellers seemed stunned as well, witnessing a robber in a ridiculous costume being kind to a lonely mother.

"You, in the New York beanie hat!" Pepe walked over to a man shaking by the fire extinguisher. "You planning to use that on me, mate?" he joked. The man smiled awkwardly, almost visibly shrinking as Pepe approached him. "You're alright, mate." Pepe patted him reassuringly on his back. "I need you to do me a favour. Stand by the entrance and keep an eye out. Don't let anyone else come in. Can you do that for me?"

"Yes, yes, I think so," Beanie hat man offered quickly, running his tongue over his mouth before moving towards the glass door slowly.

"Good, good! I thought you'd rise to the occasion. We're off to a flying start. I doubt Andy's going to be much use for a bit." Pepe indicated at the security guard who'd turned beet red.

The mother he'd been speaking to relaxed and her grip on the pram loosened. Slowly, the fear left their bodies. The tellers edged a little closer to their cubicles, peering at Pepe as if hypnotised as he marched towards them, fingers round the gun. Pepe noted the white pay-in slips strewn all over and momentarily he imagined them merging into a paper man that would become his partner, a co-conspirator who would help watch the doors and cover his back.

Pepe stood before the tellers. "You know what to do. No coins, just cash in one bag," he instructed. The tellers sprang into action shoving notes into a bag they grabbed from the floor. Once they handed the bag over they stood in a line before him. Pepe looked each one in the eye, two women and two men. They all had a slightly harassed air despite an outwardly professional appearance.

"I'm a firm believer in making work work for you and not the other way round. You!" he said, pointing at the teller called Brenda, a chubby auburn-haired woman with a red brooch pinned to her jacket. "What do you want out of this role?"

"What do you mean?" she asked, eyeing her colleagues in confusion.

"Your job. What would you like that you're not getting?"

She looked to her colleagues again for guidance, hesitating somewhat. "Erm... a raise and I don't want to do mortgage appointments anymore," she said self-consciously.

"Very good, very good. Write it down."

"What?" she asked, looking at Pepe as though he'd sprouted another baby chicken head.

"Write it down, my love!" he encouraged, he grabbed a few pay in slips, handing them to the tellers.

At this point, Andy the security guard who'd suffered

from asthma as a kid slid to the floor, wheezing in a heap, his black baton lying against his side limply.

One by one each teller admitted what they desired from their jobs before writing it down. Once they finished, Pepe addressed Brenda, the oldest of the tellers, who'd gone bright red. "I want you to hand those to your manager. Now mind! Warn him, he has to take them seriously otherwise I'll be back and it'll be embarrassing for him if I hit this branch twice."

Brenda nodded, resisting the nervous temptation to fiddle with her brooch. A CCTV camera poised in the right hand corner above the entrance whirled away, having captured the action. Pepe's gaze flicked over it, not in fear or panic, merely acknowledgement. He grabbed the bag with one hand, pulled a piece of paper from his costume pocket with the other, pinning it to the statement machine with what looked like a stick of gum. He turned to the astonished customers and simply said, "Sorry" while tucking the gun away.

"If anyone's interested, that's my recipe for coconut cake on the statement machine. Good for a day like this I think. One tip though: add some rum to it, but not too much! It really lets the flavour sit in your mouth."

He burst through the doors onto the windy street. Curious passersby watched a man dressed in a yellow chicken costume carrying a bin bag run down the road. At that point Andy the security guard stumbled up in the bank clutching his chest and waving his baton. "Call the police; I almost had that fucker earlier!"

By the following fortnight, news of Pepe's escapades had spread and he'd committed a spate of robberies up and down the country, hitting at least one branch of every major bank, each time dressed glaringly in his signature chicken costume.

After several robberies, the banking staff on duty started helping him. At the Lloyds branch in St Paul's, the staff covered the CCTV cameras; at the HSBC in Oxford Circus, two employees tied up the security guard while another kept a look out; in the Co-op in Lea, the employees had secretly been marking a calendar counting the days till he'd make his appearance, refusing to raise their police alarm when the opportunity arose. To the chagrin of the authorities, Pepe fever had begun to infect overworked, underpaid banking staff on the lower rungs and everyday innocent bystanders got caught up in his robberies. Instead of giving the police accurate accounts, witnesses found themselves misinforming the authorities, lying outright. Pepe had a strange effect on the people he came into contact with. The police began to speculate as to whether he used a kind of hypnosis to disarm people. He became a sort of guerrilla agony aunt, doling out advice to the individuals he held up, who sought his opinion on an array of matters.

"My teenage daughter's become a monster before my eyes, what do I do about this?"

"I lost my job, can't pay rent anymore; the council's given me my last warning. I'm going to be homeless! What do you suggest?"

"If you know someone's done a terrible thing, would you shop them? What if you grew up with this person and you're like brothers?"

"I can't stand my husband anymore, everyday he sits across from me at dinner I think about stabbing him with that fork. What's wrong with me?"

Pepe enjoyed these confessionals despite what appeared to be stressful situations for all involved. He knew there was a certain understanding between them. He always left his recipes behind after each one; octopus soup instructions defiantly stuck on the camera lens of the Lloyds in St Paul's, spiced pumpkin and semi-freddo dessert recipe in the dog charity donations box at HSBC Oxford Circus, a classic Hungarian Goulash recipe stuck to the cue sign at the Co-op branch. Every time after he exited those branches, the customers and staff would rush towards the doors, watching him in wonder and curiosity.

Outside a Nat West bank in Wood Green, Pepe found himself surrounded. A few police cars screeched to a halt on the high street. Several policemen jumped out, their doors slamming shut. He heard more police sirens ringing down the street, beyond what the eye could see. His body felt overwhelmingly hot, as if a fever pill had spilt in his blood, changing its formation forever. He held the Argos holdall of money tightly, feeling the strain. Sweat from his forehead dribbled into his eyes, stinging them. Pepe sensed a cold hand leave his insides, heard the whoosh of air as it pulled back then dropped. In the space between the pill melting, the bitter taste that flooded his tongue and the policemen screaming unintelligible orders at him as if somebody had pressed the rewind button to control their mouths and the sounds which emerged were scrambled, speedy, meaningless malfunctions, Pepe closed his eyes. He tapped into the feeling of invisibility that had seeped into his system for years. Tiny white specks melted in his blood. Signals in his brain transported frazzled words from the policemen to the wrong parts of his body. He vanished.

On the way, he temporarily lost his reflection crossing an unnamed planet. He left two twenty pound notes in the hand of a blind woman en route to meet her future self on the Eshima Ohashi bridge in Japan to discuss coping mechanisms for untapped potential, unrealised lives. He sat on a mountain top in Azerbaijan, unable to stop money from the holdall spilling down the side of the mountain towards confused goats jostling among each other at the bottom who wouldn't know what to do with notes bearing the Queen's face winging down, except to leap and bleat at them. Eventually, Pepe landed back in his home clinging to the holdall of cash, dizzy.

From that moment, Pepe was able to keep the police at bay by waiting for them to arrive, standing before them bright, defiant and shining. Embracing the feeling of painful invisibility, the way he had done many times in an unforgiving city, he vanished. His burden became his source of power. His vanishings left policemen stunned, reeling, clutching at nothing and questioning the plausibility of the unknown, the disregarded, the dismissed, forcing them to reach blindly for the realignment in the air. They were furious, as if their breaths and very beings had conspired against them. CCTV footage of Pepe began to appear on the News. Internet forums sprang up sharing his recipes, lauding him as a hero, a modern day Robin Hood who wrestled with the banking system at a grassroots level.

It was just after 2pm when Pepe entered the King's Lion pub at the end of his local high street. Most of the lunch time crowd had gone and there were only a few doddery old geezers who looked as if they lived in those dark wooden seats and unemployed men who'd slunk in from home or the betting shop opposite to languish in the familiar comfort of the pub. The horrendous patterned orange carpet looked about a hundred years old and the barman in the Metallica t-shirt had a copy of Dr Faustus tucked into his back pocket. It smelled of chips, beer and damp.

Pepe ordered a Guinness before taking a seat at the back where he had a good view of people filing in from the other entrance. He sank into the seat with relief, got comfortable. It was always like this, the normal part of his life, the slump. He was back to being ordinary again. It made him feel depressed but he knew it had to be this way. There was nobody he could tell about what he wanted to do and about what he'd been doing.

After his fourth pint Pepe saw himself walk into a bank where everything had turned inside out. The staff were on their knees dispensing saliva covered notes and coins from their mouths, the statement and cash machines were in the teller cubicles shattering into pieces while the alarm rang, customers fell through the ceilings wearing badges with problems instead of names; *broke, lonely, just divorced, suicidal.* The security guard held the door open while Nona floated in on her wheelchair, looking thin and sickly, clutching her knitting sticks feebly. Everything around her spun and she began to deteriorate rapidly in that chair. At each stage her mouth was made from a different object; a drip bag, a drug chart, soft purple wool. She deteriorated until she became a skeleton.

Pepe blinked and suddenly all the men in the pub were holding a failed kidney, leaking a silvery liquid into their palms. He blinked again. The kidneys vanished.

He stood abruptly. He needed a piss. He passed his image in the mirror on his way to the Gents. He was ordinary looking; sunken eyes, lean frame, gaunt face and dark shock of hair. He did not see anything special in that mirror; in fact self-loathing had become a part of his psyche, often borrowing his own voice and tongue for bouts of control, the way a virus takes over a laptop.

You are nothing. What have you ever done?

Nobody knows who you are, nobody cares about you. Nobody notices you.

If you were on fire on the street somebody would use you to light their cigarette.

You couldn't stop it, could you? You couldn't help Nona. You are a loser.

But when he put on that chicken suit that Nona had made all those years ago for a costume party, he didn't feel like a loser. And people did notice him. You couldn't miss him! He sensed himself physically growing once it was on, feeling stronger, braver and tasting the heady anticipation of sticking it to another bank.

He saw the chicken suit dangling on the silver hanger in his wardrobe, talking silently to the openings it was yet to step into. The chicken head separated from the hanger spinning towards a flooding of light, towards another resurrection, spilling yellow feathers from its mouth, passing Pepe in the mirror. Heat flooded his body; he felt the pill in his blood reconfiguring. A fizzing rang in his ears. The pill melted in his blood, tiny particles shrinking to nothing. A rush of blood hit his head, a swift high and shock followed by a sucking sound like a vacuum opening. He surrendered to the feeling. He recognised it. His image in the mirror blurred, shrouded in a sprinkling of yellow feathers. He closed his eyes. He vanished, fingers touching the vacuum just as the beer in his glass became room temperature.

Miraculously and to the amusement of some of the general public, the police made no headway in the case. Pepe's face had never been captured on screen, he never left any fingerprints as he wore gloves and he worked alone. There were no accomplices to trip him up or make the fatal mistake of boasting to others about their escapades. Pepe never kept the money for himself. He sent it anonymously to charities, stuffed rolls in the pockets of the sleeping homeless and left wads on bus seats. It felt good to be able to help people, especially those who really needed it. It felt right to compensate for what had happened, even if Nona would have disapproved of his methods. His intentions were good. And Nona always used to say, "If the intentions are good, certain things are forgivable."

Cutaways

When Nona first got sick, Pepe took an extra job to support them. He couldn't understand it, how she could seem fine one day then gradually begin to look like a stranger, with bags under her sunken eyes, her hair turning completely white and her dramatic weight loss. He was so overcome with fear and worry at the time he found himself reaching for the glass surfaces that had captured reflections of the old Nona, wanting to ask her for guidance, to stay a little longer before some other greedy, grabbing hand came for her, infiltrating the surface.

At twenty-five Pepe was cleaning offices for a living. He had attempted to get work other people would label as more decent but something about him unsettled employers. And he often answered questions too honestly.

Cleaning offices was an easy job. He had spotted the advert in a small, white box at the back of the *Evening Standard*: *Onin Cleaning. Reliable cleaners wanted, £6.00 per hour! Regular work guaranteed!*

He had ripped the page out and rung the number. A week later, he had started work. The owner, a chubby, amicable Moroccan called Amal hadn't even asked for references. Pepe had liked the solitary nature of it at first, the way you could slip through the cracks, below people's eyeline. He cleaned offices all over the city, often travelling into Canary Wharf, London's financial hub, on red buses coughing black smoke into the lungs of lost silhouettes, surrounded by glass skyscrapers winking mockingly at poorer areas just a stone's throw away.

Nona teased him sometimes, in that raspy voice of hers, "All this work! You need to find a nice girl, someone you can test those crazy recipes of yours on. Yes, someone who likes to eat with a big appetite for life, who thinks home is wherever you are."

He didn't bother to tell her that he had his eye on someone, someone he had never met and was unlikely to meet, except when he considered the possibilities in a darkened office, emptying the bins, wiping tables down, clearing snack wrappers from drawers.

In the Semtec Corporation building on the third floor, there was one particular desk he was drawn to. It sat on the open plan office boasting wide windows and a big skylight. He was convinced the gutted consciences of the city were ghosts pressing their mouths against the keyholes. The desk was grey and L-shaped. On it a picture of a walnut-skinned black woman wearing a blue flower pinned into her locks always caught his attention. It was a side profile shot and for some reason it made her seem more intriguing, like having half a map in your hands. Her head was thrown back, lips stretched in a knowing smile.

He took to playing a *Where's Wally*-like game, only with her replacing Wally in the starring role, becoming increasingly fascinated by the prospect of finding her in imagined scenarios. He saw her tucked inside a bull fighting audience, watching the bull run out of the pen into her sly smile. She was in a stream of runners at the London Marathon, sandwiched between a Pavarotti lookalike and a man wearing a TV costume. At a Staff Benda Billili concert, she was hidden inside the ceiling of the dark stage, occasionally bobbing her head down out of the shadows. Each time Pepe was always somewhere in the shot too; riding on the bull towards her, holding ice water on the sidelines at the marathon. On stage he was an extra member of the band, playing drums frenetically while she bobbed her head down into the beat.

Once he masturbated on the picture frame. She opened her plush mouth even wider when he came. Afterwards, he wiped the frame with trembling hands, feeling both relieved and pathetic. He looked up to the skylight and the foggy consciences had semen on their hands.

For a few months, he continued cultivating their fantasy life but one dank, damp evening he arrived to find her picture gone. That particular employee at Semtec had moved on. And he'd taken their girlfriend away with him.

He queried around for work, heard one of the meat shops in the area were looking for an extra worker.

"Are you squeamish? Can you chop meat properly?" Hanif, the butcher with the artificial leg, asked.

It was after 7pm, staff and the last few customers had left. The shop, a long, narrow space with a sloping, white ceiling and a red linoleum floor, seemed eerily empty. A row of display fridges ran all the way down, filled to the brim with assortments of meat and fish. More meat dangled from hooks attached to the ceiling. Behind the fridges, large wooden tables marked by blood and bones sat against a tiled wall designed as a choppy, blue sea. To the left, a lengthy, rectangular mirror hung on the wall.

"I'm not," Pepe answered. "I'm probably as capable as the average person at cutting meat, meaning not very good." He smiled, his eyes lingered on the leg jutting through Hanif's trouser, slightly smaller than the other leg. After a few months cleaning, Pepe had grown restless; it was time to move on. Nona was getting worse, one kidney had failed. She was on the NHS waiting list for a transplant but God only knew how long that would take. He needed to save money. He started cabbing at nights.

Hanif waved a bloody meat cleaver, used it to nudge some chopped lamb shoulder into a carrier bag. "The pace here is crazy. If you can't keep up, I'll have to let you go."

"Come on, I'll make you aloo gobi if you interview me!"

"You're a funny one my friend!" Hanif responded. "Offering to cook for me in exchange for an interview."

Pepe looked at the ceiling of dangling meat, threatening to swing into points of the conversation. He liked Hanif. He liked the sea in the wall that carried the low hum of fridges.

"I know what you're thinking," Hanif said, snapping him out his reverie.

"What am I thinking?" Pepe asked, keen to hear his fate one way or the other.

Hanif laughed. "My friend, you want to know what happened to my leg."

Working at Hanif's, Pepe learned how to gut chickens and clean fish properly. He mastered the skill of chopping and bagging meat in no more than two minutes. Randomly, he picked up lip reading and was able to discern an order through the din from the opposite end of the room. Sometimes, after customers left he saw their mouths rounding on words against the shop window. Words like cow leg, gizzard, goat soup. At night, he dreamt of meat resting on blue margins and chickens calmly still losing their heads, when the knife slashed their throats.

Pepe enjoyed the banter of the men behind the counter.

He grew used to the sound of cleavers hitting tables, the cash register ringing, the smell of meat in the air and small bloodstains on money notes. His recipes were tested on the team; vegetable biriyani, pumpkin pie, winter warming mutton soup.

He and Hanif grew closer; chatting over drinks at the pub, watching the world pass by during breaks from the green enclave tucked behind the shop. One day, Hanif finally told him how he had lost his leg.

"I was holidaying in Egypt. I got bitten by mosquitoes when I went in the sea then got stung by a jellyfish. I was so sick; I thought I would die, man. My leg turned gangrenous. They had to cut it off."

"Shit, that's horrible."

"Was a good holiday before I got stung and lost that leg."

A moment of silence passed.

"My grandmother is really sick. I think I'm going to give her my kidney."

"You're a good son."

"Maybe. What would you do in my place?"

"I would do the same my friend, do whatever it takes."

They sat silently for a bit, two birds leaning against a city wall with wires in their mouths.

After three months, a new meat shop opened across the street. It was bigger, busier and had better deals. Hanif began losing customers. Letting a couple of workers go wasn't an easy decision. He started forgetting orders minutes after they were made and refused to answer his mobile phone constantly vibrating in his pocket. He kept his meat cleaver close by, rubbing it on his leg, tapping it against the tables distractedly.

Eventually, he confided in Pepe: "I owed the bank a lot of money. I borrowed from some dangerous people to pay them off, but it was a trap. I'm in deep shit and the interest keeps growing rapidly."

Pepe imagined him waving that cleaver in his sleep, carving paths of escape with its wide, glimmering blade.

One blustery morning after his week off, Pepe arrived for a shift at the shop. It was 8.30am. The shutters were only half up. He walked round the back. The window had been left half-open too as though Hanif had been in two minds about something. He climbed in, moved past the freezer door and into the shop floor. Silence greeted him. Normally at this time, Hanif would be filling the fridges. The shop was virtually empty; most of the stock had been cleared out. Pepe's heart rate increased. Only the fish in the fridge facing the display window still harboured night in their eyes. He headed back to the freezer door and opened it: it was also gutted except a few dangling chickens.

He grabbed his phone from his pocket, nearly dropping it, and rang Hanif. The number had been disconnected. Edging forward, he bit back a groan, shivering slightly. Hanif had cleared out, closed up shop. He was still owed a month's wage. He needed that money. How could he have taken off like that without telling him, without warning? He knew things had been rough, but he felt betrayed. He felt sad and alone.

Pepe leaned against the wall. The cold meats hung from the ceiling in a haphazard circle. The room swayed. He could hear the sound of the streets coming to life. He noticed the chickens dangling had purple bruises on their bodies. As the bruises spread, the chickens lifted their heads. Pepe stood again in shock. One by one, the chickens leapt off their hooks and stumbled towards him, bloodied rims around their necks. They placed their beaks inside his head and began to chatter.

Pepe came up with a plan. Nona needed a kidney transplant urgently. He would give her his. He was sure he'd be a match. They couldn't hang around hoping to be bumped up the waiting list anymore. They would do it privately. He'd heard of such operations happening in other countries. He'd fly Nona out to India or somewhere else and get it sorted.

The house now harboured a funny, stale smell and Nona struggled to breathe. He read to her at nights from Alexander Pushkin's Eugene Onegin, lifting his head occasionally from the page, watching the faint smile on her face, the light shrinking in her eyes.

He hit every major bank asking for a loan. "It's urgent, please. I'm not sure what else to do." The responses were variations of the same answer:

"I'm afraid you don't qualify for that kind of loan."

"Your credit rating is really poor."

"Without any steady income the bank can't take that risk, cabbing at nights isn't enough."

"But this is an emergency," he wailed.

"I'm sorry, sir, we can't help you. Good luck!"

A week later, Nona passed. He experienced a pain in his side so sharp, he had to stay in bed. He drank himself to sleep. In the morning, he woke with a fury that consumed his whole body. He'd tried to do the right thing but where had that gotten him? He remembered the chickens talking to him in Hanif's freezer and the costume up in the attic, waiting to speak its own language.

A month passed, and Pepe lost his ability to vanish. The robberies stopped. He was ill. He shuffled around the house, feeling hollow and thin. He could barely keep anything down. Looking in the mirror, his reflection was missing. He began to search round the house for it. Something was changing within him that he couldn't explain. He felt like his organs were failing. He was sure of it. Something was happening to his kidneys, he'd seen it in the pub weeks back. They were shrinking inside him, reappearing in the hands of those men in the pub who rubbed it over their mouths.

One morning in November Pepe visited a Barclays bank as a customer, without his chicken suit persona. He stood in the queue running over his options. Like Nona, he would be left waiting to die. He could feel himself getting sicker by the day. There would be nobody to look after him. Instead he'd have to sit in his lonely house surrounded by things he couldn't take with him to the other side, the stench of illness in the air, dreaming of headier times when he'd had the courage to leave his mark, longing for the embrace of a lover. He'd think about that pretty woman he loved to place around the city and how he'd hoped to run into her one day randomly, just like that.

He thought of his chicken costume in a casket slowly filling with soil and began to cry quietly. An Asian customer service woman in a neat uniform approached him. He noticed her long, black hair brushed her shoulders and her clean fingernails.

"Can I help you?" she asked.

Pepe opened his mouth but couldn't speak. Instead, choking sounds emerged and a small, yellow wing fell out, landing on her left shoe. They stared as it slid further down her shoe. As he pulled the gun from his pocket, a piece of paper dropped out. The woman gasped, stepping back. The queue scattered. Pepe checked the security cameras were on before facing her again. He placed the nozzle in his mouth and fired. The shot rang loudly. The air left the room. As Pepe's body fell, people dived for cover, terrified.

When the police arrived, they found the customer service assistant crying over Pepe's lifeless body, holding a yellow wing in one hand and a piece of paper with a recipe in the other, entitled *Dia De Los Muertos Queso Fundido*.

Footer

She wanted her feet fucked. She wanted the soles kissed, arches traced, toes glistening with saliva. She knew she had good feet, beautiful in fact. Free of corns, blisters, scars and all those horrible afflictions women experienced from years of squeezing worn feet into heels. An old lover had told her so in bed one day. He'd held her shapely size 6's in his hands as if they were pieces of art, softened them with his breath. "Your feet are amazing," he had said, visibly dribbling. "They're little women, little Botticelli Venuses." She had succumbed to the feeling of being worshipped, to a delicious, deviant unspooling attached to a man's tongue flicking between her toes. That was how it had begun.

She placed the ad on Craigslist, listing the things she wanted. She imagined her golden, stiletto heel pinning down a man's lip and her feet curled in anticipation. Loneliness watched from her sky blue Ikea sofa. It was three months old, had a green head, blank human eyes and a crocodile's tail. Its body was mushy, lacked any real definition and looked as if it would sink into itself. Three months ago it had accosted her on the escalator at London Bridge and now it refused to leave her flat.

A few days later, she checked her email. She was inundated with responses to her ad.

Oh God, let me smell your feet, CHARLES KING P wrote. *Keep them smelly, wear sheer tights and rub them on my face.*

I want to fit half your foot in my mouth, make me choke on it! I love the picture. You have pretty, brown feet, from ZICO 99.

Will you kick me in the balls? They'll turn the same colour as your dark, purple nail polish, from AMPERSAND MAN.

All you have to do is let me pleasure your feet. If you like, you can chain me like a dog and I'll lick them from my pathetic corner while they're propped up looking down on me. You deserve it, from MARTIN P.

One by one, she read their requests. Those men were like her, beautiful, defective bottles standing on a ledge. Loneliness moved towards the large living room window as she read. Wagging its tail, it watched the jagged light filtering through. She threw an empty bottle of Moscato at it. It dodged, surprisingly deft, then shrank back and chewed on bits of broken glass. It was its second meal of the day.

She worked for 44668, a mobile text and answer service. Her job was to answer questions on anything and everything. *What's the rarest orchid? Do dogs dream? Will swallowing a teaspoon harm you? Can you die laughing?* Between responses, she researched on the net or cut out pictures from old magazines to stick them on her collage board. Once or twice a week, she polished her feet and oiled them, admiring the sheen they took, as if under the soft focus light of a camera.

She met the first guy, ZACHARY LIKES TO DANCE, in the evening at an empty park in Holloway. They convened in the play area. She laughed internally since he seemed the opposite of his moniker: gangly, awkward and sweet. He smelled of cigarettes and had a bald patch. His long, tapered, organ player's fingers trembled slightly. The left sleeve of his black, woolly coat was frayed. She had the urge to tug that thread to the street, into a cluster of people and leave it lying there like a dead weed. Instead, she asked if she could draw on a part of his body.

"That's a strange request," he said.

"No stranger than what we're about to do," she retorted.

He agreed. She fished out her blue biro and began to draw a blueprint on his bald patch of a place that had no name.

Afterwards, he buried his nostrils in her sweaty feet and inhaled. He grinned, hot breath warming her toes. He came up and she continued sketching.

"That feels oddly soothing," he said.

"I know," she answered. "These lines need to come out."

Later, beneath the shiny slide that looked like an aluminium slug in the darkening light, he took her stockings off gently, kissing the birthmark on her inner thigh. He kneaded her feet, held them to his face, licking the day's trail. He told her that the year before he'd had a diving accident in Turin. He'd smacked his head against the side of the pool. Floating in the water, he'd watched his blood curl into a ribbon. And the last thing he'd thought of before everything went dark was that he needed to reach for it to tie that ribbon of blood around something dodging him in the water.

He ran his fingers over her soles and whispered against them, "If I could eat your feet, I would." She felt high, as though sitting on a folded edge of paper in the sky, legs dangling over. The park became acres of green with her legs planted in the soil, multiple versions of her feet bending in the breeze.

She cried on the way back home, watching car headlights fall on carcasses telling bedtime stories to dirty bonnets. At the flat, Loneliness was perched on the couch, mouth open and blinking at the television screen. She held the semen-speckled handkerchief of ZACHARY LIKES TO DANCE up. Loneliness ambled over, swallowed the small, white material whole, tail wagging. She sat on the couch, carrying the creature on her lap. She recounted the day's encounter out loud to it, stroking it, remembering her fingers on ZACHARY's bald patch, his keen mouth on her feet sucking greedily, and then asking, "Please can I come on them? Please can I have your panties?"

Instead she'd seen his handkerchief tumbling in the void inside her, along with other items that had landed silently. She'd shoved one stocking in his mouth before he buried his nostrils in both feet, inhaling deeply, hands grabbing, asking to be suffocated by them repeatedly.

Loneliness, somewhat sated, fell asleep.

SABIEN X was an art tutor. Brown-haired and golden-eyed, he possessed an inquisitive, long face and aquiline features. He talked with a lisp, as though a small, slight silhouette passed a limb through his teeth with each word uttered.

In his roomy studio, the large canvasses leaning against white walls were their audience. There were two windows, one overlooking the street and the other above a pathway leading to the garden of headless stone gods, whose heads sank in the green pond. The smell of paint and dampness hung in the studio air. She caught smudged purples, pinks and reds on a handful of paintbrushes in the sink. Coloured fingerprints on a half-empty jar of water on the table edged into a hand.

"Recently," he said, "I have begun collecting stuffed animals."

Awkward introductions wrapped up, she placed her bare foot on a stacked wooden shelf, beneath the gaze of an owl and the spine of a thick book on the lost architecture of ancient Rome. He crawled towards her wearing just a black scarf, hypnotised by her feet as if a murky horizon unfolded from them. He placed her foot on his chest. She felt his heart beating against the sole. He closed his eyes, held her foot still, finding a rhythm. She ran through the canvasses, borrowing their painted skin.

He told her, "Lately, I've developed a taste for eating uncooked food. The other day, I ate half a packet of sausages raw. I don't know where this has come from or why I'm telling you." She nodded because she understood the arrival of things you couldn't explain. His uncertainty blurred the lines of his body. At home, Loneliness left holes in the black scarf, SABIEN's gift to her.

The third guy, RAY, a country boy from Devon with sleepy brown eyes and broad, reliable shoulders, was a farmer at heart. Still adjusting to being in the city, he felt out of step with London, with its pace. RAY had first discovered his sexual pull towards women's feet aged twelve when in the summer the blue Volkswagen Beetle of a group of young nuns driving past broke down near the farm. While his father was taking a look at the car, the nuns had slipped their sandals off. Something about them being covered up except for the exposed skin of their ankles as they danced in the field, their pretty bare feet in the dirt, had caused a twinge in his groin. RAY had stared at them standing by the tractor in wonder, in discovery. He had masturbated that night. He had fallen asleep thinking of the nuns in the tracks on the field, light pooling at their heels, their arched feet eluding him in the dirt and him trying to catch them all at once with his mouth, tongue, hands.

After a year in London, RAY had begun to grow things on pillows as if they were soil. Sometimes, his lovers would wake to find offerings by their heads: a weightless ball of pomegranate seeds, a blue turnip, a stalk of asparagus.

They would laugh uncomfortably. "Why have you left

a vegetable on the pillow? What an odd thing to do!" One day, a lover had risen to discover a fragment of a future he'd grown overnight, a sleep-lined model family made from cabbages. She had fled, leaving the cabbage family to wilt on the maroon bed sheet.

At his ramshackle attic space, RAY cried against her feet. Embarrassed, he confessed it was the first time in a while and that something about them made him feel both desire and vulnerability. He ran ice cubes along the dips and curves. Her collages were stuck between the wooden beams in the ceiling, talking to her in a muffled language. She groaned back at them, pointing her toes from the ice strokes. Words in rigid blocks of ice travelled along her soles: *She gathers, she draws night siblings, breaks skin, hollow instruments to mould with one breath.* Then ice and words became a small, cold river. Four words melted last: *She gathers, she draws.*

In a rhinestone-studded belly, she caught maps of places yet to exist. Her pen leaked. RAY grew a potato the shape of her foot. Afterwards, he sucked on the corner beneath her fifth toe, where the skin was tougher. An ache migrated when she came. Her tiny silhouette broke into a memory in his iris.

At home, Loneliness growled in greeting when she collapsed on the sofa. It flicked the television channels. Later, it chased her potato foot through a gauzy revolving door.

In April, her mother Merlene arrived to stay for a week. Merlene had a stout frame, perfect cinnamon-coloured skin and a soft voice with a hint of an Antiguan accent. Typically, she appeared unannounced, wielding a small black suitcase. At the front door, she looked up from heavy-lidded golden eyes, busied her fluttering hands smoothing down a floral, pleated skirt. "So this is where you been hiding, girl."

"You should have called first," she answered, conscious of still being dressed in her pajamas. "I'd have cooked something." She drew Merlene inside, closing the door and leaving the short chain to rattle in protest against the wooden doorway. Her mother's scent of rose clogged her nostrils.

Merlene studied the flat with critical eyes; the stencils of shadows on orange hallway walls, some stilettos with broken heels strewn over the floor, a cramped kitchen housing a rusty Indesit washing machine, the recently wiped sink. She ran her fingers along the dust on the TV set. Merlene ignored the feelings of guilt and disappointment coursing through her veins. She knew things about her daughter that Grace would be surprised by. She had the eye. That was why she'd come.

She spotted Loneliness licking itself in a corner. "That dog needs a bath, Grace," she commented.

"It's not a dog!" Grace shrieked, feeling tension creeping into her neck.

Merlene shrugged her black woollen coat off. "Good, I was about to say it's the ugliest dog I've ever seen."

Loneliness growled.

Later, Merlene unveiled her favourite memory: teaching Grace to ride a yellow bike aged eight. It was tucked into her suitcase, folded carefully between clothes. Together, they watched eight-year-old Grace ride through the rooms, laughing on her bike. When her eight-year-old self ran out of breath, tired from riding for hours to keep the smile on Merlene's face, Grace tried to slip one leg of a broken shoe onto her foot, but of course it didn't fit.

Two days into her stay, Merlene and Grace continued circling each other.

"You need a different job," Merlene said. "I don't know why you call that… creature Loneliness or why you insist on drawing bad things to yourself."

"It's just a name!" Grace spat.

"It's not healthy for you to be cooped up working indoors, not interacting with people."

"I have friends I see."

"I know you don't, you've always been awkward," Merlene retorted, mouth a grim line.

"I'm not awkward."

"You used to be a lovely girl."

The words echoed in Grace's head, prompting a memory to resurface. Her sixteenth birthday, a gathering of excitable girls playing games, hands tied behind their backs eating cake from the table. They had played spin the bottle and truth or dare laced with gulps of rum. Icing had crumbled on dresses. And of course Merlene had appeared, walking on crumbs of cake barefoot. Crying after the party had finished, "You're not my little girl anymore, Grace." It had been said with a hint of malice. She had realised then that Merlene had never wanted her to grow up.

All week she tried to entertain her mother. They took in a play at The National Theatre about a homeless man who believed he was God. They cooked together, argued over what to watch on TV. At one point, Loneliness escaped with the batteries from the remote. Merlene wrestled them from its mouth. Grace couldn't see any foot worshippers during this period. She couldn't gather. She knew Merlene would smell it on her. Each night, she watched Merlene perform her ritual of rubbing rosewater into her perfect, smooth feet, then carefully wrapping bandages around them. Each time Grace's resentment grew. But she didn't ask. They never discussed it.

At the end of the week, she accompanied Merlene to Waterloo Station. They embraced, surrounded by a backdrop of swirling commuters. She almost asked then, but Merlene shut her down, as if she knew. "I nearly died giving birth to you, girl." The gleam in her eye hardened before she disappeared down the platform, gliding along on those bandaged feet. Grace found the nearest toilet, collapsing on the seat in tears.

Spring arrived and Grace woke one morning to sunlight streaming through her window. A cool breeze caressed two shadows in her gold curtains. They yawned, stretching tongues made from a woollen coat sleeve. She felt an ache in her leg. She peeled back the duvet to discover her right foot had grown three times its size seemingly overnight. She squealed in horror. Not only had it tripled in girth but it had lost its beauty. Gone was the appealing arch, kissable dip. Now it was deformed, twisting slightly to the left. There was no way she could gather with this affliction.

Over the following weeks her foot continued to grow, until it became like a giant's foot attached to her shapely, well-proportioned leg. It showed no signs of stopping, looking larger in doorways as the days passed. She felt ugly and freakish. She stopped going out and checking messages for her ad. Loneliness escaped as she threw the bins out one day. She was no longer nimble enough to catch it. Her foot had to be dragged around. Her collages abandoned her to become background images in the lives of others. When she cleaned her room, she found a bottle of rosewater in the bottom drawer. It wasn't until the cap was twisted off that she tasted tears on her tongue.

One evening, she flicked the TV channels to BBC News. A sharply-dressed male broadcaster in his fifties announced the police were investigating a series of sexually motivated disappearances they believed were connected.

When the men's faces flashed on screen, she felt a tingle of recognition. She remembered their hungry mouths on her soles, licking, sucking, mapping, absorbing the undetectable poison from her feet, her inheritance.

In her mind's eye, she saw Loneliness growing on the escalator at London Bridge again. Fat with all the evidence she'd fed it, strumming the old shape of her beautiful, lost foot like an instrument.

Disconnected, Grace mourned her old feet, mourned the feeling of being worshipped. She thought of those men, recalling each one. And she remembered standing barefoot on the tips of silences winging their way over to the bodies.

Nadine

I make electricity with my brain, enough electricity to power laptops and start kettles boiling.

A mouse had eaten the sympathetic expressions of the doctor who diagnosed me when I was fourteen. He told me I was epileptic and had "grand mal seizures". I didn't know what was so grand about them. I just felt like I made a show of myself. Slipstreams showed me eyes rolling in my head, spittle dribbling down my chin and uncontrollable jerking. I used to pretend spirits borrowed my head to see things. After they finished, I'd wake up.

Now at twenty-six, I get auras before a seizure. It's like intermittently having fucking déja vu. On a bad day I'll do anything to avoid my aura: shove it in an old, tattered bag, dump it in empty cereal boxes or my DVD player so it can run. On a good day, I'll embrace it like a favourite jumper; try to take sly pictures of it with my Nikon camera.

Coming out of a seizure is terrifying. I know I've visited the green sea where those who regularly die temporarily go. It has a floating white bed sheet of charts, tracking all the comings and goings. But what do I do in that sea for the two, sometimes three minutes—the average length of my seizures? I can never remember. My body always feels heavy, as if I've been carrying a washing machine spinning possible cures for epilepsy, sinking down into the sea, kicking fervently to save the cures. I always cry after my seizures, green sea water trickling down my cheeks. The faces of my family hover above me, etched with concern. I grab at them as if they're lifelines floating out of my reach.

Except for a couple of interlinking roads breaking them up like referees, all the houses on my street are attached. The English are too efficient with space, to the point where, just to get some freedom, your home may one day end up on a football field, in the park opposite the swings or on the cold shoulder of a motorway.

When I hop out through the front door that early afternoon, the sky is swirling moody hues of grey. Tracey Chapman's crooning in my earphones about a fast car and the Nikon camera on my neck is ready to snap all the injuries of the coming week. My fat, auburn twists bob up and down.

A couple of steps down, I spot Elora, one of our neighbours, with her fifteen-year-old granddaughter Nadine. Elora is a stout woman and her short hair neatly packed into a small bun is shot with grey. She still has her Jamaican accent. She is the kind of woman whose shoulder you grab on to steady yourself. Nadine has Down's syndrome. She has that slightly vacant look people with Down's syndrome carry, but when she hugs you, she means it. I jog up to catch them.

"Carpe diem," I say.

"Cree!" Nadine's laugh is soft and warm. She flings her arms around me. Between the dormant static in my brain and the squeeze of her fingers, we're Einstein's secret equation.

I thread my arm through hers. "You guys checking out the international food fair at the store car park today?"

Nadine is wearing a Lauryn Hill t-shirt, blue jeans and white Nike classics. Her hair is separated into pigtails and tied with a red ribbon. Elora picks up the pace. "Yes, we're making Guinness punch cake. You OK, darling?"

"All good. Guinness cake sounds intriguing," I reply.

Nadine says, "Beer in the cake!"

I steady my bag. "Beer in the cake should be our new mantra, Nadine. Save me a slice, alright? Nice outfit. Oh! Stop one second." I aim my camera, snap Nadine and her red ribbon. I run ahead scattering kisses behind, yelling, "Keep some Guinness cake for me. Beer in the cake!"

I photograph the things I see. Body parts of a rabbit reassembling on the eastbound platform at Mile End station; the man pulled aside by security at HMV Oxford Circus as a naked redhead crawls out of his rucksack; the guy whose right hand is a gun and has to take the bullets out at night so he doesn't shoot himself; the sky at night. I look for God's face in those images. He is the Big Foot of the skies.

When I arrive home that evening, a police car is parked opposite Elora's house. Some neighbours are out chatting. Elora emerges, trailed by two uniformed officers. She looks grainy, as if she's been sitting in a TV screen. She is frantic: Nadine has disappeared.

My sister Dakore is a wisp of a woman who sleeps with books on her bed. She pads about the house in old T-shirts. An unapologetic slob, my mother refers to her side of the room as "the hovel". When I'm bouncing around early in the mornings, she cracks a sleep-lined eye open, muttering a variant of "Jesus fucking Christ! You're like a wind-up toy that doesn't run out of batteries!" Then she pounces, smothering me in kisses.

My younger brother Scoli is a genius. He studied animation at Ravensbourne College and draws funny little characters. Tall and handsome, he has vampiresque molars he inherited from our mother and a scar on his left hand. When he's having intense periods of creativity, he listens to Joana Newsom on loop, her haunting voice lingering in our hallways, the musical equivalent of a Grimm's fairy tale.

I've been having panic attacks since a terrible thing happened to me two summers ago. When the panic hits, I make my way to Scoli's room. He opens the windows, sits with me taking deep breaths. Sometimes he fetches me a cold apple to bite on. Afterwards, I hear the apple in the corners of the house, damp from the green sea, bruised from the thing I cannot breathe through.

Three days pass. I wake up with Nadine's laugh in my chest. She still hasn't been found. There's no media coverage because they don't care about missing black girls. The only exception is our local paper, *The Recorder*, which has used the picture I took in their article. I know Nadine's alive. Each day, I look at my picture of her. Each time her expression changes, from lost to forlorn to angry. She's sitting in the corner of the frame, her back turned and the red ribbon on the floor. Her legs are dangling off the edge as if any day now, she'll fall out of her own picture.

I leave the house armed with copies of her photo, my camera and a voice recorder I bought on sale at Argos. On my way to the small shopping complex in Beckton, I think of Nadine and how sweetly she trusts. Her collective handshakes have been driving cars at night. They are driving not to places or cities, but to the next promise, the next time someone gives their word.

The small complex where our local Asda stands is stunted. Maybe the original idea was for something bigger but the budget fell through. We have Asda, Hamil's Internet café, a post office/shop, the music store, a chemist/opticians and Shoe World. Everywhere you look there's unfulfilled potential carrying the residue of lead from sketched lines. I talk to staff at each store but there are no real leads. I put pictures of Nadine up on their walls.

Each time someone asks, "Why all these questions? Shouldn't you be leaving this to the police?"

I don't bother telling them Nadine is my friend. Instead, I say I'm a trainee journalist with CNN and it's my first investigative piece.

"You mean I could make the news?" That stops the fuckers asking questions. I picked up this trick from my sister. She tells elaborate lies and never feels bad, as she believes that lying often is the humane thing to do. Sixty percent of the time human beings interact they're lying to each other. It's a coping mechanism.

I talk to Sammy at Shoe World who gives me good deals through his staff discount. There's a beautiful sheen to his dark, Ghanaian skin and I can still hear the tiny hint of a lisp when he talks. This makes me like him even more.

"Sure I saw her," he says. "It's hard not to notice them. They're always together. I remember her ribbon."

"What about it?" I asked.

"She was retying it. It must be a lot of pressure looking after a kid like that."

After three hours talking to locals in and around the centre, I leave, wondering if the inanimate objects saw more. Maybe the red post box opposite the music store had a blueprint of every scene etched on its pile of envelopes. And the fat blue change machine could cough out silver trails of her movements.

I talk to Elora and she trembles, sitting back in the large, wine-coloured sofa that dominates her living room. She is thinner. If I touched her with one finger, her legs would probably buckle. She left Nadine in the yoghurt aisle briefly, asked her to get her favourite brand while she grabbed some vegetables. That was the last time she saw her.

At home I study my yellow post-it note board of evidence. Every sighting leads to a dead end. I move things around to think fluidly. Nadine in the newspaper picture frame stands up and looks right at me. My head is full of cotton wool, stopping thoughts from connecting. My skin is static, my hands jerk involuntarily, and my body follows. I know a seizure is coming, running erratically towards the heart of me.

When I come round, my sister's holding my hand. She's changed one grimy alpaca T-shirt for another of Grace Jones.

My brother cracks a relieved smile. "We've run out of apples," he simply says.

Wherever she is, Nadine's voice has planted itself in my eardrums. I keep going over evidence, thin accounts that are different textures of clothing; Nadine retying the ribbon in her hair, waving at Brenda on till thirteen, weighing melons in the fruit and vegetable aisle, flying through the exit. One tiny thread could mean something; I just need to know what it is.

Wednesday arrives grey and groggy as if on flu medication. By evening, everybody else in my house has gone out. I fall asleep early and dream of Nadine and I dropping down a tunnel like coins flicked in. Eyesight is a neon glow and things hurtle down; the BMX bike I had at age nine, the globe in my room, Nadine's Lauryn Hill T-shirt, her ribbon, the yellow post-it notes with my handwriting scrawled across them. It all becomes ink tears on square paper suns. When we land, Nadine leads me to my green sea, to the water's edge where reflections of others are back to back. Her voice erodes the lines of their bodies.

I wake up to a panic attack; *call an ambulance!* In the van their gazes switch on small light bulbs under my skin. At the hospital waiting room, I'm not the only one having a panic attack; all the elements of my dream are too. We take up an entire front row.

My sister picks me up. At home she tucks me into bed. When her back is turned, I fish out the tape recorder containing interviews and my observations on Nadine's case and press play.

At 8.30am my phone rings. My tongue feels like it's done five rounds with Ali. The white display screen shows *Number Unknown*.

"Hello, Cree?" a male voice with an Asian accent asks when I decide to accept the call.

"Who's this?" I reply, ready to pretend it's the wrong number in case it's a sales call. The voice breaks slightly—my room has shitty reception. "Sorry, who?"

"Hamil from the Internet café! Listen, I remembered something about Nadine. I think it's important..." His voice trails off.

"Stay there, I'm coming right now."

"Do you think you could come around 2pm?"

"Hamil, Rome was probably built before 2pm. Don't go anywhere."

I grab my trainers. Every word I'm saying tastes foul. Sweet sleep can leave dead gifts on your tongue. Hamil is still yakking away. I think of Nadine's screams being parachutes in the sky. Static from the phone threatens to suck me in. I face Nadine's picture in the frame. She's alert, leaning forward; a flame licks at each heel. She's ready to fling herself into the whites of my eyes.

At 9.00am the Internet café, a long narrow room with dull decor, contains six people. It's amazing how many monitors these café owners fit into small spaces. The café has stout, black chairs you can swivel in, maybe into another place or outcome. Monitors flicker and I see hands pressed against the screen from the inside, but this could be a trick of light.

Hamil has the smallest head I've seen on a man and a faint moustache that changed its mind about its own density halfway through growing. His movements are that of a park squirrel on acid. Blink and he's at the opposite end of the room fiddling with a loose wire, convincingly slipping an international calling card into your clutches or pressing his hand against the buzz on the right side of my brain to stop the bee inside from wailing.

We sit in the tiny kitchen at the back with the door shut. An old monitor is on the table. Hamil knows my face. When the Internet was down at our house for a month, I practically lived in his café.

"Hamil, do you like Egg McMuffin?" I lay my tape recorder on the counter; switch it on and split one Egg McMuffin.

He crumples his face. "Half an Egg McMuffin?"

"I never share Egg McMuffins, you are an important man. So you remember something?"

He takes my offering, chews a chunk. "Yeah, the thing is, you see someone many times, one sighting blends into another."

"What are you saying? Help me out, it's early."

He demolishes another mouthful in true park squirrel speed. "I see her and the grandmother all the time. They shop like everyone else. But she knows him; I've seen her talking to him a few times."

"Who?"

"That kid Ryan and his buddies. I think they go to the same school. You know him?"

I shake my head. He chucks the McDonald's packaging in the bin. "Mixed race kid, good-looking, wears a maroon Umbro jacket. They both attend St Michael's."

"How do you know this?" I ask.

"I run an Internet café. It's amazing the bits of conversation you catch, the things I know about the locals; websites they frequent, if they use online banking and with which bank, when their last job was from printing CVs. Anyway, this Ryan kid and his mates come in here sometimes."

I lean further back into the counter. "What's he like?"

"He's a regular teenager, confident and popular. The girls like him, except..." He pauses for a few seconds. "...he's a different person when you catch him alone."

"In what sense?" I ask, realising a shared Egg McMuffin isn't enough for breakfast.

"Thoughtful, sensitive even but hides it. So he and his friends are talking to her and I don't think anything of it because I've seen them chat before. Then, some woman calls me over about a virus and she's out of my head. I just assume she went back into Asda."

My fingers reach for the recorder. "Ok, that's good, thanks."

"Oh, one more thing, these kids were bored. The food fair was on and not really their bag. They were hanging out, drinking Budweiser and Guinness. I found this," he said, clicking into a shared folder on the screen.

"What is it?" I ask, zipping my bomber jacket up.

He drags a file from the folder into the centre of the screen, clicks on it. "I only stumbled on this because I was clearing files out this morning. It's a Skype video of Nadine on her last visit here. Somehow it was accidentally recorded."

Nadine's face fills the screen. She's laughing with that innocent, blank eyed stare and I want to cry. I feel myself welling up. The voices of several boys behind her fill a void. Their faces float into the screen; they look young but have hardened gleams in their eyes. *These boys could be my little brothers*, I think. A sick feeling grows in the pit of my stomach.

"Come on, Nadine, come for a walk. We want to show you something."

"Don't you want to be like the other girls at school?"

"Beer in the cake," Nadine says.

"Yeah we'll give you beer, you stupid cunt." They snigger, the screen flickers, they all become grey. Nadine gets out of her chair. The screen flickers again, shrinking the boys' faces in what feels like a second.

"You think you'd recognise these boys?" I shove the recorder into my pocket, from the slightly open door I can see more customers have appeared at the counter, waiting for Hamil.

"Yeah," he replies. "I'd know those little bastards."

I launch myself at Hamil, planting a kiss on his cheek. "Next time you're getting the full English, the works."

He flushes, delighted, but moans, "You owe me five quid."

"Put it on my credit!" I yell, breezing through the door.

"I don't do credit! Not even for a beautiful black girl who knows how to use her wiles!"

All I could think about were Nadine's last words to me— "Beer in the cake"—and the boys' faces closing in on hers on the screen.

I find Ryan at his mother's, hitting a punching bag in the garage. There are weights on the floor, dumbbells, a weighing machine, an area for chin ups, sealed boxes around the edges. I feel as though I've entered a makeshift ring, both of us orbiting towards a scene where the other is floored. He is melancholic, serious, polite. He offers me a glass of water. I decline, despite knowing I will need water during the break, against the ropes. He meets my gaze slowly. There is both relief and fear on his face. "I wondered when somebody would come." The punching bag dangles between us.

Once upon a time, the wolf inside a boy fell in love with a girl's expression; fell in love with its innocence. The boy held it between his teeth when the wolf sat on its haunches. The girl's name was Nadine, the boy's Ryan.

Ryan's unwitting seduction began under the umbrella of rusty school gates and the grey wheezing of winter. Ryan started to notice things, such as the girl's ripening body and the effect her pure smile had. He saw beauty when superficiality told him he shouldn't. Beauty drew itself into the placid lines of her face. *This is wrong*, he thought, *she's not normal, people will talk! They'll laugh.* Nadine wasn't like other girls. He wrestled with the wolf.

He walked her to school a few times, talked about the silent things he'd never had the courage to share. He watched them fall on her face as she listened attentively. People sniggered at her holding his blazer in the hallways, during breaks. "Look at that spastic," his friends mocked him. "How's your disabled girlfriend? Do her yet? You freak." And the wolf laughed, *Hahaha, should have given her to me.*

Ryan looked at other pretty girls but he found most boring. They talked about silly things. He waited for them to say things of consequence but it never came. Yet he could be himself with a girl whose limitations were inescapable. There was something darkly wondrous about Nadine, about all the things she couldn't say or express that intrigued him. He wondered what those things were. He started to resent Nadine for his attraction to her. The wolf ruptured something in his blood.

On the day of the international food fair, he and the boys were at the shopping centre, all six of them drinking and getting high. They spotted Nadine wandering on her own. Ryan waved her over. She babbled about beer and baking a cake. They hung around in the internet café for a few minutes since Mark needed to Skype some French girl he'd been chatting to. When they left the café, Ryan gave her some Guinness. The boys offered her more beer, a little weed. They chuckled when she sputtered.

Their smiles became one white trap. They passed an invisible note between them but nobody knew whose handwriting it was. Ryan threw his arm around her reassuringly. They took her to the Alps spot with its hidden enclaves and view over the area. She was yanked deep within it. The unnamed flower inside her nursed a fist growing through blood. The boys held her down, undid their trousers and ripped the red ribbon from her hair to wrap around her fate. Two doves died in her eyes as they put a bag over her head. They took turns stealing her virginity. Their hands splayed, covering sprigs of grass that sprang up as witnesses. The wolf won and the boys howled at her face, the bagged afternoon moon.

Thanks to Ryan's confession, the police are able to find Nadine where they left her, naked and circling her footsteps. Traumatised, unable to speak.

According to the judicial system, the boys aren't adults, so nobody knows what sort of sentence they'll get. CNN does a feature; they call me an intrepid sleuth. They offer me an actual investigative journalism internship.

Nadine's picture stops moving in the frame. I keep it in an old tuck box. I visit her a few times and just talk, even though she never responds, except to squeeze my hand. I tell Elora that the old Nadine is still in there somewhere. I know what it's like to have a terrible thing happen to you and hold you by the throat.

September arrives. The air is crisper; leaves bend to the will of the wind. People's walks change. I haven't had a seizure for over a month, which feels great. I'm still sad about Nadine, mourning who she used to be. I'm sad that we never see monsters changing their disguises. Sad that teenage conformity can be a knife to the skin and that unspoken things can take the shapes of wolves and men interchangeably.

It's that time of year again and the local businesswomen of Sure Start Network are having their annual event. It's a good gig for me: I chat, take pictures, get paid. My camera is safely packed in my bag and I zip through the front door.

I pass Elora's house on my way, look up to my brother's bedroom window. His head bobs slowly, appreciatively to music. I hear the sound of my cold green apple making its way to his grip. Nadine's face swims in the glass. Tears run down her cheeks. She silently begs me not to forget her. I hear her.

I nudge the squeaking gate open and slip a card into the post slot for Elora and Nadine. Light falling on the pavement makes me contemplate possibilities. I think of standing beside Nadine on dark slip roads connecting the incidents of that summer, of the boys' tongues leaving their mouths to become small, thirsty creatures in the distance. I imagine waiting patiently until Nadine starts to speak again.

My head feels funny, murky; the wind is cold against my face. My right arms jerks. Something's running towards the centre of me, digging its heels in. The world outside opens and I fall into it.

Poko, Poko

Sun-soaked yawns hover in Sal Island, Cape Verde. Desert land, miles and miles of barren spots unfurl in a series of lithe morning stretches. Our hotel Porto du Vento in Santa Maria, where my sister and I are staying, is rustic and warm. I like that we're the only guests, and that the white woman who runs it writes but can never decide which language to write in because she speaks two—Portuguese and Spanish. I like that she eats with her staff and that they never have most of what's on the menu. The special is the same every night: rice with chicken and potatoes. Her huge, black dog drools while we eat and her adorable mother hovers in the background of our live pictures. Her curly silver hair bounces and she wears neat, flowery shirts. She offers us cake or biscuits after breakfast and fills the iron with water to wipe frowns from my clothes. She is so cute and quaint, my sister and I pretend she's a mafia don hiding out in Cape Verde. She has the look of a woman who would surprise you with tales of her life.

There are building works outside the hotel and surprisingly, this doesn't annoy me. I enjoy being in the centre of things, among real life, real people, circling the hem of developments just through our daily walks. This is Africa and it's hot, but not unbearably so. The dogs and cats here are lean. They catch sunrays on rooftops and take shade under cars. The guardians of the streets, they bark and meow across to each other at night.

Cape Verdeans are ridiculously good-looking people, effortlessly so. It's a wonder they don't start the day gazing at their reflections for long periods of time. The cab drivers are all young and attractive, as well as the shop workers, the bar staff, the fishermen. Even the local beggars are blessed with nice looks. The people amble across roads in slow, even strides saying, "No stress, no stress", the motto on the island.

The streets in Santa Maria are all connected and dotted with brightly coloured houses. At times I see silver scarves trembling but they are freshly caught fish winking at me from wheelbarrows. The children playing are drops of blood on hot tarmac, bleeding into one another.

Charming Senegalese shop owners wielding Colgate smiles accost us mid-stride. They show us pictures of their newborn babies and talk of family back home. I can't help it, I find myself reaching into my wallet to buy turtles carved from wood and jewellery.

Boys on the cusp of manhood carry surf and skim boards under their arms. The taxi drivers in light blue cars with yellow stripes shout at us, "*Espargos, Espargos!*" We shake our heads, slightly embarrassed to be among black people and still be easily identifiable as tourists.

My sister and I are crossing a wide, thirsty patch of ground two minutes from our hotel. The gates are cactuses the length of my legs. Aluminium drink tabs are its scattered teeth. We spot a silver van with the company name in Portuguese followed by tours in sweating black typography. Forty-five minutes earlier, I'd booked a tour of Sal with a man who came down especially to the hotel. The driver honks the horn. He's looking right at us.

"You think that's our guy?" I say, turning to my sister. She's wearing an orange and purple patterned blouse that looks like a female orgasm. Her red braids are flammable. She is a match, femininely pretty with tomboy swagger.

"Maybe," she replies noncommittally.

I move my shades an inch further back down my head.

"He fits the description."

The van pulses, hums. I take another look at the driver.

"Shit, that guy is really good-looking," I exclaim.

"You've been saying that about everybody since we got here. What, are you surprised or something?" my sister quickly replies.

I suddenly feel too casual in black Ali Baba style pants and a blue and white striped vest, £2 from Primark, bikini peeking from underneath.

"No, but that's our guide?" I wonder.

We're closer to the van now, two lenses meeting at the same point. He nods at me, a brown-skinned black man in his mid-to-late twenties. He's wearing a white baseball cap backwards. And sure enough, he's the best damn looking driver/guide I've seen in a long time.

"*Ola.*" My voice is the sound of a car engine warming up. "Are you our guide on your way to pick us up from Porto du Vento? *Obrigado.*" In one sentence, I use the extent of my Portuguese vocabulary.

He doesn't lean forwards towards us but back into his seat. "*Sim et sou ging para escolher as pessoas para cima do Porto du vento para uma turne.*"

A fat fly buzzes near my ear then hovers in the car window as though it will translate. I throw my sister a look she pockets.

"Shit, this guy doesn't speak English," I say. He chuckles. It is rum sloshing over the rim of a glass.

"Small, small," he replies, holding my gaze. At that point I wonder if his whole arm will cover the span of my rubber band waist, if he's a prime or even number. I wonder if the probability of my forehead leaning against his chest will make us an oblique triangle wearing two pairs of sandals.

My sister folds her arms, cocks her neck to one side so it looks like a tipsy exclamation mark. We start firing:

"What's the name of the tour company you work for?" (Even though it's boldly emblazoned on the sides and back of the van.)

"Show us your licence."

"What parts of Sal are you supposed to take us to?"

"What's the name of your boss?"

He holds Portuguese and broken bones of English as his bullet proof vest.

"*Sim, muito bon.*

"*Existem mais pessoas?*

"*Vamos ao Porto du vento para pegar o resto.*

"*Eu nao me entendem.*"

He fishes out a map of Sal and hands it to us. I recognise it; it's the same map the man I booked the tour with showed us. He simply says, "Zecca."

"Yes!" I wave my arms like a conductor whose specialty is conversation. "Zecca is the guy, he's your boss."

"*Sim.*"

"This is definitely our guy," I say and my sister's arms unfold. We hop in, me at the front, she at the back. He turns the ignition and we set off. Above, someone has spilt orange paint in the sky. Tyres crush the skeletons of scenes just gone. People are specks crossing my irises. A man on a donkey with a bored expression meanders along on the other side of the street. The van stops outside our hotel.

"No more people," I gesticulate. "Just us, understand?"

He nods his head and smiles warmly. "Yes, understand."

The seat feels hot against my bum. I slot the metal seatbelt tongue into the red throat of the buckle, making a French kiss. I twist in my seat. My sister is already gazing out of the windows.

"Rock and roll," I say.

I notice he has two very long fingernails, unusual for a man. The white cuticles are stark against the black steering wheel. I find it slightly creepy but curious. At that length, it's obviously a choice to keep them that way. Maybe he plays an instrument, the gunibri with its body made from a tortoise shell. He plucks at the strings feverishly after hours on the road. Or he's a world record holder for untying Gordian knots. Maybe he uses it to snort coke during breaks from June to September; white, hot reprieve from idiotic tourists yammering on incessantly at him.

I point to his nails. "Those are way too long. You should cut them." I make two fingers like scissors and aim at his hand before angling for his head.

He looks at me, slightly bemused. "No."

I think he finds me a little strange.

"You like them that way?"

"Yes."

"Why?"

He launches into a short monologue in Portuguese. I nod and smile, without any idea of what he's talking about. The next day's dawn cracks on my face.

In Ponta Preta we stop at a stream that ripples from the breath of Gods. Weird rock formations resembling life-sized wisdom teeth surround it. The water is murky aqua, coloured by thoughts from all its visitors. My sister and I roll our trousers up. We wade knee-deep into those thoughts. They rise to the surface in the shape of weeds, leaves and debris. My hand is a sieve scooping them. My sister splashes water on me, catching me off-guard. I squeal and splash back. He stands to the side laughing at us. His laugh is a winged thing circling above. Our water fight soothes the dry air. We run out, dripping onto hot pebbles. My sister wanders to the left where a strip of concrete dusted with wet moss hair leading into the stream awaits. I weigh a pebble in my hand and chuck it in as far as I can. It fails to skim the water. My sister is on the strip now, at the end where the water greets it. She slips and falls back. Her head smacks against the concrete. We rush to her simultaneously. I fuss in older sister mode.

"Are you okay? That looked nasty."

He helps her up, asks if she needs anything.

"I'm fine," she mumbles, looking a little disorientated. My sister is epileptic and I worry about any falls or accidents involving her head. I'm panicking that her brain may be dislodged somehow, floating in her cranium like a pickled egg. She dusts herself off.

"Want me to take you to a hospital to get it checked out?"

"No, it's okay, it's sore that's all."

He walks ahead of us, we slip back a bit and I whisper, "I'm glad you went first and not me. I was about to do the same foolish thing!"

She cuts her eyes at me. "Bitch. Your concern is overwhelming."

We wander over to a large square area that must be nature's chessboard. The rock formations are eroded, rugged pieces. The sun makes its moves in the day and the moon at night. Play continues eternally. We are momentary reserve pieces hopping in between them, fingering rough grooves and jagged edges. After the last thoughts from the stream air dries on our toenails, we drive on. The van swells with heat you could mould into extra passengers. Soukous music blares low from the CD player. The aircon blows cool at my ardour crossing its legs.

He tells me his name is Lindo. For some reason it makes me think of the game Connect Four. But instead of slipping blue or red circular chips into patterns of four, I'm slotting aquiline nose, nearly black eyes, stubborn chin and hairy wrist. Diagonally, horizontally, vertically.

On the way we see the huge rock that has a lion's face staring into the horizon. I wonder if it roars unexpectedly sometimes, if embers from those roars sneak into the right side of chests so it can beat too, bits of rock breathing inside people.

I notice he honks his horn at many passersby. He seems to know every other person. At Buracona natural springs, he takes us to a small area between the rocks that looks like the entrance of a cave lying on its back. The water is so far down, if you were to fall in you would surely never get out. It's dark in there but a part of the water is jarringly bright blue, it's a jewel worshipping the light catching it. My head feels queasy. It wants to vomit at the prospect of accidentally falling. We navigate our way to the other side of the springs where people can swim. The routes are steep and tricky; he helps us through, holding our hands. His touch is warm and lingers even after he lets go. I'm fairly athletic but pretend to be clumsier than usual.

My sister rolls her eyes and grins at me. "I see you," she murmurs.

"It's working," I reply sheepishly.

A man with dreads repeatedly dives from the top of the rocks, attacking each effort with gusto. A white couple swim with their baby. My sister and I dip our feet in. Our bikinis are second skin. It irks a little to watch the corner of the scene unfold and not sink our bodies in. Lindo motions at me. "No swim?"

"Nah," I shrug. "I'm not a very good swimmer and my sister can't swim."

I'm consoled a little by his look of disappointment.

At Pedra Lume, the abandoned ships from the 1800's

cave into one another in a misshapen embrace of rust and decay. They miss rough seas and rougher captains, the days of sugar transporting. They are no longer beautiful in the harsh mirror of day. I can't afford to pay for both of us so I send my sister through to explore. Lindo and I drive round the back to watch her become a dimple in the distance. We lounge in the van next to each other with the doors open. We talk and laugh, two people discovering something old showing its new face. Our gaps and silences are empty rooms to sit in. We swap numbers. We colour our fingers with so much more.

On the way back we visit the mirage spot, a river's reflection beckoning. We are children of the dust leaning against the wind's hold. The closer we try to get, the stronger the wind becomes. Eventually we turn back. The wind uses our clothes to slap us.

Sal Island is a different animal at night with its yellow bulb glow. It is occupied by people as well as moods; joyful, raucous and reflective. On our two dates, Lindo and I walk around Santa Maria holding hands. Our shadows use our words to make maps on the soil.

Making love on a beach is not romantic. Sand gets in my hair, bra and bloodstream. My head becomes an antenna to spot passersby. The bolstered boat shielding us from view feels like it will set sail on sand. The moon's silver light smile cracks the sky. I'm forced to make sand gloves with my palm so I can't stroke Lindo's hair. He dips his head and sucks citrus from the inside of my arms. His saliva is a spell of rainfall becoming night dew on the mounds of my chest. His two long fingernails are magic markers drawing on skin. He spits the pips from my watermelon tongue. Liquorish coated words travel through the tunnels in my ears. The frothy waves greedily lap at the dusky breasts of the shore. He buries the condom in the sand. I tell him his sand baby will punch its fist through. It will uncurl it and hold the green veins of our night up as an offering.

We don't say goodbye. Our goodbyes dwell in the clammy pockets of Santa Maria, watching love fevers perusing fresh victims.

At the airport the plane takes off, altitude and air intertwining in a sport nobody has bothered to name. My intestines are sucked through ash clouds that are airborne cigarette stubs. I'm mourning not what was, but what could have been, a well of emotion that shifts between the shallow and the deep. I wish I didn't fall in love with beautiful looking men with two long fingernails and slow smiles like light flickering. I wish my heart wasn't broken in three, with one piece browning on a barbecue, another lodged in my ribcage and the third a boy floating on out on the waters between the islands. I wish this white aeroplane was a big foam bed to cushion the fall to reality.

A tear drops on my cheek. I'm sure Lindo is driving his silver van inside it, clearing the salty liquid away with the windscreen wipers. My sister clutches my hand. I turn to show her my back, my skin of picked seams that has come undone.

Please Feed Motion

On the third Thursday of each month, before writing to Eros, Nesrine Malik, prisoner 2212 pulled skin from the thing living in her throat. She performed this ritual without fail and had done so for four years since landing at Woodowns prison on drug charges as an accessory with intent to supply.

Nesrine had arrived with a few items; an afro comb, a brown leather wallet and two first class stamps. It was love that threw Nesrine in jail. Blind, dangerous, destructive love for a man who'd groomed her to be his soldier on the streets. A man who'd told her there was wonder in her infectious, hypnotic smile and who liked to rub his thumb on her palm, slowly in an anti-clockwise motion.

Emerico had only ever visited her in prison once and only to inform her he wouldn't be coming again. "This is how it is," he had said, watching her coldly, dispassionately, the chunky gold chaps bracelet on his wrist so large it knocked against the wooden table with the slightest move he made. He had been wearing his fade neat, his boyishly attractive face had remained distant, the proud flair of his nostrils had roused in her the memory of having pressed her lips there.

At his declaration, Nesrine had slumped in her uncomfortable chair in shock, shoving her hand into her braids, heart-shaped face hollow, crumpled, looking through the glass partition, wanting to press her mouth against the smattering of holes there to get some air. It was a different kind of air that he'd brought with him.

When he had gotten up to leave, she was vaguely aware of the sound of his chair scraping back, of the ceiling fan spinning, slicing her protest-laden tongue, of the other prisoners' heads bent towards their visitors, deep in conversation. And then the jangling of the guards' keys, dipping, and falling into the darkness of her throat.

Then everything changed. Nesrine wasn't sure whether it was the sticky heat of the room, the worn edges of the cheap brown linoleum floor that was starting to come unstuck, the sound of the glass door sliding open slowly, mechanically, or the boom of her own silence as that man left her to rot. Something changed in the air. The prisoners' faces stretched, distorting into caricatures in the afternoon light, leaving their bodies to float in the dusty windows, crying at personal items they recognised spinning in the distance. Visitors' hands rummaged through their pockets, searching for things that had fallen through an anti-clockwise gap. Guards scrambled on the floor, sniffer dog collars around their necks, dodging batons flying at their faces.

Trembling, Nesrine stuck three fingers down her throat, convinced something would emerge from the moist darkness. While she grabbed at the thing there, Eros, shaking with anger, appeared for the first time in the empty visitor's chair opposite her. Tears ran down his cheeks. Stunned, Nesrine removed her fingers from her throat, leaving the thing in the dark screaming. She saw Eros had only half a beating heart, shrinking and swelling in his chest. He set his bow and arrow down on the floor. He pulled Nesrine through the glass partition so she could breathe. The cuts around her mouth did not matter nor did her deadened tongue. He had come.

*

Nesrine sent the postcards to Piccadilly. They never came back. She imagined them flying boldly on the wind. That year, Nesrine sent Eros postcards of skeletons floating in the abyss. Before that it had been lost cities and prior to that it was women inventors. Without fail, every month she made a different prisoner press the damp tip of their tongue to the corner of the postcard. They always grumbled but nevertheless indulged her.

"This is stupid, still it doesn't cost me anything so I'll do it."

"You are bonkers. Eros is something somebody created. He's not real."

"You're not asking for juices from my lady parts which would be more worrying yet frankly, somewhat arousing."

Nesrine knew he was real. She'd touched him, been rescued by him. She'd seen her pain and destruction reflected in his face. He'd caught her when she thought her organs had absconded from her body to become small explosives beneath the fingers of other prisoners.

She fed Eros snippets of prison life; that Hollis, prisoner 4712, was found dead in the underground tunnel trying to escape, surrounded by empty crisp wrappers, rats eating the last images from her eyes, how Moffat, prisoner 3083, had fallen from the ladder injuring her shoulder whilst building the set for their interpretation of *Much Ado About Nothing*, how Gaudier, prisoner 2241, still possessing a hint of her French accent was found in a donkey costume screaming in the costume wardrobe, waving a large candlestick holder at anybody who approached. She told Eros about her diary, which she kept tucked away beneath her mattress.

At night, Nesrine ran her fingers over the kink in her hair, along the expanse of her brown skin where tiny scenes from a life lost rose to the surface mimicking the shapes of small countries. She thought of Emerico's deceptive face. It only ever came to her in parts; left side first then the right. Never head on. How like him that was. Even in absence, he didn't show you the whole picture. She watered his face with tepid prison tap water. She cried trying to silence his overarching, growing mouth. Sometimes she dreamt of emerging from a white triangle in the dessert, holding the remnants of her battered heart to an abandoned bow and arrow.

On February 8th 1995, Nesrine's postcard to Eros was delayed because of the netball game. The cold court was covered in invisible scuff marks from black, worn, plimsolls and the prisoners seemed malleable; blink and they'd be babies in orange and blue team bibs scrambling for the ball while the prison cat Homer kept trying to shove its head through the hole on the left side of the court, wanting to observe this grey world from a different angle as the women transformed. The locks in their chests clicked open, airborne bodies slick with perspiration, catching other things than the ball. Homer tried to leave a paw print on the game but the flashes of blue and orange were too quick. Too sly. Too seductive.

Nesrine flew around the court in her position as goal attack. She felt she could be anything, such was the feeling of exhilaration, of freedom; a magician's chest chasing its tricks, a concert reveler crowd-surfing the wrong way, a microorganism outgrowing the confines and gaze of its microscope. Hot on her heels was Harris, prisoner 2214, who played centre for the opposition. At the edge, where the half-circle surrounding the goal met redemption, Harris knocked into Nesrine with all her body weight. Nesrine fell, then sprang up like a prize fighter already tasting the spoils of victory; an extra packet of cigarettes, the title of Woman Of The Game, a chance to order two books of her choice at the prison library. Nesrine shoved Harris back. Their mouths curled dangerously, the way mouths do when words harbor small, sharp instruments that glint silver amidst their snarls.

A guard acting as referee blew the whistle, but it was too late. Harris grabbed a yellow-handled screwdriver from her pocket, stabbing into Nesrine's throat in one quick motion. The din rose. Nesrine fell to the ground, hands on her throat as blood spurted. Her legs jerked. Homer's head shot out of the hole. Harris was dragged away by the guard, her pockmarked face beet red, her buzz cut defiant in the air. The court erupted. The other prisoners dashed into the centre. The two teams fought, turning on each other, ready to leap off the court and take a different warpath through the trembling goal net.

Nesrine bled into the crack of joy redemption had offered, then cruelly snatched away. There would be no postcard to Eros that month. Having escaped, bearing a puncture wound in its head, the thing from Nesrine's throat stumbled in the light of the grey world, winded, in search of another moist home.

Five days later, just past 10pm, the statue of Eros hopped off the top step at Piccadilly, clutching Nesrine's final postcard. His head fell, the pain in his chest was so intense he thought it would split him in two. He felt sad and powerless. He knew there would be no more postcards to intercept from the bright angles of the morning. His footsteps were heavy on his way down as Piccadilly Circus buzzed around him. Huge, brightly lit billboards blinded from all directions beaming *Sanyo! TDK! Coca-Cola!* The concrete steps usually heaving with bodies were fairly empty except for a homeless man curled up in the middle of the bottom one.

Morning arrived and cradled Eros sitting on a park bench cold against his back his hands, turning over Nesrine's postcard. Anger rose inside him, pulled the corners of his mouth down. His limbs had a stiffness he needed to walk off.

A plan took shape in the white curls of the clouds. He decided to head to Leicester Square where the statue of Charlie Chaplin awaited him. Charlie on his stone plinth was splendid in his signature tramp ensemble, right hand wielding a cane.

Eros hopped onto the plinth, placed a hand on Charlie's shoulder and settled his cold lips on Charlie's ear, whispering, "I need your help, I've lost someone. The half of my heart I have left can't bear the pain, unless I do something. I need you to keep my spirits up." His voice cracked.

Charlie's lids flickered; he wiggled his fingers, made an "Ahhh" noise as he spotted a lone man in a blue windbreaker barking into a phone.

Eros grabbed Charlie, holding up the postcard. "This is what I have of her."

Charlie read the postcard, a wistful expression on his face. "I can see her. I can feel her spirit. Can I tear a bit of this off?" he asked, ignoring the increasing noise of the city coming to life.

"Why?" Eros asked. "you didn't know her."

"But you've shown me a piece of her so I want it too."

Eros nodded. Charlie ripped the left corner off and slipped the piece into his pocket. Eros took the postcard back. "That's the prison address." He pointed at Nesrine's scribble in the right corner. They both stared at the postcard as if it would transform into a blind, winged thing.

Charlie took his hat off, scratched his head. "I know what you're thinking."

"I have to get something that belongs to me now."

"Who should come with us?"

"Let's ask Nahla. Nesrine mentioned her in an old postcard. She never got to see her."

They jumped off the plinth. The grass surrounding them went bald. The pigeons shedding their grey for the pavements began to peck at each other frenetically.

Eros and Charlie travelled on to Stockwell Memorial Gardens where the statue of a black woman stood. Nahla The Bronze Woman. Ten feet tall and holding her baby boy high above her head. Her gift to him was flight. On the ground, there would be ways and means to deny him this. She told them she'd already traced the shapes of Nesrine's lost dreams. She too tore a piece from the postcard, slipping it beneath her tongue.

Next, they stopped by the Vomiting Fountain Sculpture. His white lips and hands trembled to life as he was handed the final piece of the postcard. His dark, misshapen body was rough to touch. He heaved then; yellow bile from his throat coated the pavement. On they went, the Vomiting Sculpture catching all the ailments Nesrine was yet to have experienced, a revolving door of sickness; the flu she would have gotten in the early part of the year aged twenty-seven, the thrush that would have had her rubbing small blobs of Canestine cream on the brown-pink folds of her vagina, tonsillitis. The sharp stomach cramps she'd have gotten from food poisoning, the vomit from her stomach as a result. The Vomiting Statue inherited these illnesses that would become poisonous black mushrooms with bulbous heads.

The statues continued as a group. They marched on, creating a flurry that swept over the city. People pointed, fascinated. Some brought out their mobile phones to take pictures or film them. Others touched their faces and bodies gently, as though they were made of porcelain. Staring as if the earth they knew had tricked them, as if anything or anyone could take on a different corporality and come to life.

Over the next five hours, they made their way towards Woodowns Women's Prison on the outskirts of Chelmsford. They trekked across motorways, bridges, through underpasses and along bike trails. Now and again, they stopped for breaks; drinking from brooks or park ponds, watching their reflections' mouths glimmering in the water.

The statues arrived at Woodowns at 10pm. The prison sat on a lengthy, remote stretch of road. A few rusted lampposts along the grey tarmac looked like pitiful light bearers from a bleak dystopian future.

The statues fished out coins they'd borrowed from a supermarket coin machine. They placed them in their mouths, swallowing heads or tails as they edged closer to the prison, a large brown bricked building. There were no barbed wire fences surrounding it or huge gates as one might have expected. Instead, there was a circular parking area for visitors and a big green sign bearing arrows and directions to the various blocks. A white water fountain sat just outside the closed reception area. They took turns drinking from it, watering the coins inside catching fragments of light from the day. At the top of the road was an old, abandoned post office building, boarded up and decorated with patches of graffiti. Several minutes from the prison, a bowling alley closed for a few months for refurbishment had a neon sign that read *Welcome to Walley's!* and a winking, red-headed woman shaped like Jessica Rabbit leaning against the exclamation mark.

The statues continued, the particles of a tiny planet assembling inside them. Several steps behind the fountain lay an underground tunnel leading inside the prison, hidden by a heavy, circular metal lid and copper bars that bore the imprint of frustrated hands that had had to turn back. Eros pulled the lid off and the Vomiting Statue prized the six bars open slowly, one by one. They entered the tunnel, assisting each other as a cold shaft of air welcomed them. It was dark, dank and bore the smell of rot and the echoes of things lost. The Vomiting Statue threw up, then pulled from the sick a red ruby stone that shone brightly to guide them. On their left were some wires covered in blood. Crisp packets floated on the thin layer of dirty water on the ground, rats scurried into the silvery insides to eat reflections of themselves. The footsteps of the many plucky prisoners who had attempted escape, running to meet their doom, had long faded. Holding those bars angrily, they'd cried as the injuries in their blood became small creatures leaping through the bars' gaps, into the world out there beyond them.

The statues heard these echoes as they made way, knocking torches with batteries that had failed to fuel the last legs of escape, scooping floating matchsticks missing fires consumed by the cruelty of fate. Eros began to whistle Tracy Chapman's "Talkin' Bout A Revolution", one of Nesrine's favourite songs. The other statues joined in. It travelled through the air, into the ears of prisoners in Block B, who slowly uncurled their bodies from their bunks, listening intensely. The statues left the tunnel through its exit on the exercise court of Block B; drab, grey and boasting two netball goalposts at either end with nets that trembled, having caught the many daily conversations that slipped into cracks.

A cardboard sign reading *No Banned Items* allowed blew onto the court. Charlie Chaplin took over holding the ruby, signaling the others, placing a finger over his lips. He spotted the thing from Nesrine's throat raising its small, slimy arms towards them. Charlie took his hat off, scooped it up. Phlegm-coloured and sickly-looking, it pointed at the building by the side of the court.

They followed the building round, till they found

themselves at the entrance of the smoking area by the guards' hub which had been left open. Inside, a small cluster of guards sat before CCTV screens, watching them intermittently, batons on the table, blue shirt collars undone, keys hanging from slack belt holders. Relaxed in their glass cubicle, the guards had not spotted the statues' slow infiltration. There was no camera on the court and therefore no feed to pick them up for two to three minutes, allowing a good window of time to make their approach. The CCTV footage flickered as though being interrupted. Two guards snoozing at one corner table were left unaware. The other two keeping watch were eating doughnuts and drinking watered down cups of coffee.

Eros and Charlie Chaplin leapt through the glass into the cubicle. Bits of glass showered the thing from Nesrine's throat, like diamonds shimmering over a small mutant. The guards jerked in their seats, shocked. Two guards spat out mouthfuls of doughnut, scraping their chairs back quickly, spilling coffee on their uniforms. The others had woken abruptly, drool drying on the corners of their mouths and yelled, "What is this? Stand back! You're looking at serious charges for this."

The CCTV screens flickered again, playing footage of prisoners from the cameras' blind spots; scratching their faces in the showers, deliberately burning their hands in huge pots of tasteless soup they'd stirred till the ache in their shoulders began to travel to other parts of their bodies, crying over pictures of loved ones that had changed somehow over time. The statues ushered the guards into an empty cell, locking them in, swiping their keys.

The prisoners of Block B started to whistle loudly, knocking their bars insistently using shoes, books, stolen cutlery, pipe bars, their limbs poised in excitement at what was to come. The thing from Nesrine's throat led Eros and the other statues to Nesrine's now empty cell. It sat on her dented bed, leaving a yellow stain. Eros raised the mattress till the thing was perched at an angle, lifted Nesrine's blue diary from beneath, held it tightly. They left Nesrine's cell, opened other cell gates. Female prisoners flooded out, bedtime wear rumpled, waving their items like flags.

"This is crazy!" one prisoner yelled. "Who are they?"

"It's Eros, Nesrine did this! Another answered. Nesrine made this happen."

The prisoners stared at the statues in wonder, then started to chant, "Nesrine, Nesrine, Nesrine!"

They charged at the statues. The thing from Nesrine's throat ran amongst them, growing stronger from their energy. A heady shot to the puncture wound in its head. Its limp wrist pulled the echoes of Nesrine's laughter and the tip of a screwdriver scraping a thorny bottom. Eros ushered everybody back onto the court, through the tunnel and out onto the street. He raised Nesrine's diary in the air which spawned a fresh burst of chanting her name from the prisoners. They jostled amongst each other, excitement building, their chatter rising. The statues led them to the bowling alley; they broke in through a back window. They flicked the lights on, filling the building with brightness.

Prisoner 1046, Sunny Whittaker, in for GBH switched the CD player on. Prisoner 2017, Delilah Armstrong, in for armed robbery took a group to the lanes where they separated into teams bowling with glee, sliding their bodies down on the floor, throwing the balls with abandon. Prisoner 2246, Arlena Mattieu, in for murder led another group to the games room. They took turns leaping on the trampolines, stretching their hands out to smaller versions of themselves running through the lights, holding bits of debris from the lost scenes in their lives. Another group surrounded the snooker table, shooting coloured balls into the mouths of ghosts.

At the lanes, the prisoners waiting to bowl exchanged their favourite memories of Nesrine; like the time she organised a sports day of ridiculous activities after spending weeks convincing the governor to let her do it, or the year she arranged a secret Valentine's evening where the prisoners could be each other's dates and exchange cards and gifts they'd made, or even the annoying way she always had to beat everybody during their exercise hour on the court in the mornings, covering it so quickly, as if something she'd built the night before was chasing her, high on some unidentifiable fuel. They celebrated her. They broke the vending machines, staining their tongues with Skittles and warm chocolate.

The statues started to whistle again. The music changed. The Ronnettes' "Walking in The Rain" blared from the speakers. Everywhere, the prisoners danced; in the bowling lanes, at the slot machines, on snooker tables, by the shoe lockers, at the trampolines, by the fake lottery machines where the balls looked like black eyes. By now, the ruby stone had been passed to Nahla the bronze woman statue; it sat gleaming between her breasts.

In the early hours, Eros and the statues led the prisoners into the streets, down dawn's memory of the night before.

Having fallen in love with Nesrine the moment her heart broke, Eros held onto her diary as though salvation lay within it. Bits of corroded flesh gathered within the void in his chest. He read the pages in sly concrete gaps longing, wanting, crying, while the thing from her throat now powerful, uglier, spilled bits of another earth all over the city.

Anonymous Jones

Published in the letters section of the defender website, 04/05/2007

Dear all,

This is why I hate endings. Sometimes you don't get to choose how the story goes. I was fired from my job two years ago. Soon after it happened, my then-boyfriend ended our relationship with a single sentence: "I'm not sure I want to be with you anymore." I honestly couldn't think what put him off. Was it because I often pretended my life was like a badly dubbed kung-fu movie? Or that I once admitted to responding to an advert in the paper for female wrestlers when I was low on cash? Or that I still had my invisible friend from age five as a twenty-four-year-old? It seemed short-sighted and a shame to throw the friendship away.

I shared my innermost thoughts and secrets with this man. I told him about the school camping trip when a classmate accidentally set my hair on fire playing with matches (luckily our teacher had a bottle of water in her bag), that I was once hospitalized for three days after winning an extreme chilli eating competition, and that the words levitation and abracadabra make me happy because they're loaded with possibilities.

We broke up the day I got fired. For that extra cruelty, for his incredible knack of bad timing, I dreamt about holding his head up to the windows of restaurants filled with unsuspecting couples warning, "Don't believe a word out of each other's mouths. Your good intentions mean nothing!" It wasn't only the way the relationship ended that made me angry, but also the point at which it happened in my life. I worried that my Alsatian dog By Golly Wow would be the only good thing left in my world. He's a funny dog, he loves listening to The Stylistics which is why I named him after their song and he howls whenever fireworks go off on New Year's Eve. He curls under my feet while I watch TV and keeps me company during restless, late night walks.

The job I was booted from was charity fundraising. Funny I got fired from a job I had only taken as a last resort. Bizarrely, people treat you like scum when you're a street fundraiser and marginally less so when you do door-to-door work. I'd been doing residential sign-ups. It was really hard work, we had to deal with cold conditions, unpredictable weather, being on your feet for five to six hours at a time and the constant reality of turning up to work to find half of the team had been fired or quit. After a slow start, I improved rapidly, hitting and surpassing daily targets. I had more doors slammed in my face than I ever imagined. My favourite rejection came from a cranky guy in his late thirties: "Is this another thing for kids in Africa? I'm sick of being made to feel guilty about that with the constant bombardment of adverts showing these kids with flies around their mouths! I don't give a shit about that right now. My wife just left me. Someone should donate to my charity. How about that? Mike Edwards: I need some help. Now get lost."

Three weeks into the gig we were on a road in Earlsfield, the team spread out; my supervisor Jaruk a couple of doors down from me. I was chatting to this woman who must have been five or six months pregnant. I wasn't sure if she was taking the bait since she had steel in her eyes. Usually, you can tell within the first two minutes of a pitch whether someone will sign up for a monthly donation but I couldn't gauge her. She invited me in. She seemed fairly well-off; she wore a striped Monsoon maternity dress, the floors of the house were wooden and the ceilings high. The living room was large and tastefully decorated with a fireplace and some expensive-looking china in a cabinet. A painting hung on the wall of a really old white man with an elaborate moustache dressed in a suit, who looked as if he could keel over any minute.

I was giving her my winning spiel but throughout I was actually dying to go to the toilet. After six minutes of persuasion, I couldn't hold it anymore, so I asked to go and left my stuff against the sofa. Three minutes later, I came out only to discover her casually riffling through my things, my wallet in hand.

"What the hell are you doing?" I asked, trying to snatch it back, only for her to reply, "Give that here!" with no shame whatsoever.

The next thing I knew, I was struggling for my own wallet in someone else's house. It was like being in a nightmare. We fell against the sofa wrestling for the wallet, knocking some of my stuff over in the process with the man in the painting still fingering his walrus moustache, his expression that of a bemused observer. She started screaming that I'd kicked her in the stomach. I had to call Jaruk over. She claimed I'd stolen twenty quid from her mantelpiece, my own twenty pounds! She was like a professional actress in front of Jaruk. She stood trembling and tearful with just the right amount of panicked distress on display, heightened by the fact that she was pregnant. I had to call on my better angels to restrain myself. As Jaruk dragged me out of there, I told her I hoped her child had webbed feet.

The charity fired me. They said I had to "re-evaluate" my

attitude to charitable work. But I didn't do anything wrong! What kind of world do we live in where someone attempts to rob a charity fundraiser? I despaired at the darkness around me.

I went back to the drawing board. I have a degree in Communications, which is about the most useless degree you could have. In fact, the paper it's printed on is probably worth more. At least with an English degree you can always teach; an admirable profession in my eyes. Teachers should be given way more credit, good teachers change lives.

I signed on for a bit but the system is designed to make you feel like something stuck in the sink plughole at every stage of the process. And the money wasn't enough for a church mouse to live on. I tried applying for a local council job in my borough but failed the maths test. I was depressed for a while; I struggled to get out of bed some days. When I did, I'd sit by the living room window smoking cigarettes and listening to old blues records, By Golly Wow circling my chair, licking my left hand consolingly.

I worked as a waitress at a greasy spoon café for two months. I actually liked the customers well enough, particularly some of the builders who loved to banter, wearing unfailingly bright yellow jackets, boots covered in cement, hard hats tucked under their arms or on the tables besides steaming cups of tea. They would often tease and compliment me. I couldn't help being interested in their stories. What some considered an underwhelming job seemed magical to me; the ability to create something from the ground up, something that didn't exist before, which would breathe, live and buzz with human activity. They were building a new spa roughly five minutes away from the café. Sometimes, when I got some spare time, I'd imagine myself in the windows of that building, picking up instruments I could use to carve a path in my own life until I found the right one.

The fact that there was only one waitress per shift meant that it became really stressful when the café was busy. Hal, the manager, started trying to touch me up, which was awkward to say the least. In the end, he told me he had to let me go due to "unforeseen financial circumstances." He decided to keep the other waitress, Moira, because she'd been there longer. I was less angry about losing that job, maybe because I felt I'd gotten something from it. The customers liked me, people weren't mean to me the way they were during my fundraising days.

I signed on again to buy myself some time. That lasted about a month, since I kept missing appointments. I considered doing voice work since I did a great Frank Spencer impression, a good Cilla Black and an excellent Moira Stewart. I left messages for companies that never called me back.

Then I started working for a sales company selling perfumes on the streets, commission only. I mostly took the job because I needed one. I was sure that had I walked into that interview a blind, one-legged, black dwarf they'd have given me the job anyway. I did that for a bit until one day the company folded, every trace of them gone. I was stuck with a box of cheap-smelling perfume I wouldn't have been able to get rid of at a bazaar.

Once again, I had no money and possibly a terrible run of bad luck. The day I found out about the company, I dragged that heavy box of perfume home. I called my sister Vivian crying. I fell into a hole, I couldn't recognise myself there.

It's hard being a young person these days. There's so much expectation to do the right thing. What happens when you keep trying to do the right thing and it keeps backfiring? What happens when you feel invisible and lost, that nobody cares? You apply for jobs on the lower rungs of the ladder since everywhere you look people are silently showing you that dark girls like you won't be allowed a seat at the table. I drifted in and out of jobs because I never discovered what I was good at, because nobody ever helped me find out as a kid. And Viv did the best she could after our mother went back to St Lucia when I was nineteen.

Dear all, really I wanted to say that I joined the army. I know, it surprised me too. Maybe it wasn't such a good idea but it seemed like it at the time. I needed structure in my life. I was tired of drifting from one thing to another. I miss Viv, her bawdy laugh, the flowers she always tucked in her hair. I miss By Golly Wow. I miss the musty smell of him and the way he's always excited to see me in the morning.

I've seen some crazy things since joining the army. Just two weeks ago, there was a bombing in Basra and one of my fellow officers, Louise, got killed. I saw the lower half of her body blown right off. Witnessing people die this way impacts you. I can't stop thinking about it. I can't stop feeling that heat, the splinters in my eye, the smoke all around, the sudden weight of my uniform, the deafening screaming, the desert threatening to swallow me. I can't stop feeling the panic in my chest and seeing a grenade exploding from Louise's stomach in my nightmares. I still remember the picture she showed me of her son playing football with the watermark on it. And I cry when I think about it. I cry when I think about her.

I miss London. I miss home. Being out here puts everything into perspective. That's what I wanted to say. Everything seems small and a world away. It's like my vision is bloodshot now and I can't get rid of the blood no matter what I do. I can't stop thinking about my endings, all the ones I can remember, whether or not I had much of a choice in most of them and if that makes me feel any better.

What I really wanted to say is: find what you like so you

don't get the wrong ending. I don't know how to tell my mother that I left one war to join another in Iraq. I'm scared every day. British troops here are under constant attack, they're bombing us on the roads, firing rockets at our base. I'm going back out there tomorrow. And I guess I'm writing this letter in case I don't come back, in case I never get to write another one again.

Yours Sincerely,
Anonymous Jones.

The Thumbnail Interruptions

"I kissed a mouse once," Jonno said.

They were lying in the park, their backs on the grass looking up at the sky.

Birdie saw a road in the sky where God was distributing throbbing headaches to dysfunctional dreams, but she didn't mention this. Instead, she retorted, "How do mice kiss? With or without tongue?"

"Very funny. I was fourteen. We put paper traps around the house. You know? The ones you stick glue on, because suddenly they were everywhere, eating holes in our underwear, gnawing through cereal boxes, scratching relentlessly in the attic. Even daring to come out and watch TV with us!"

Birdy laughed. "So what? You formed an attachment to this particular mouse?"

"No, it was weird because for weeks the traps weren't working. They caught other things: my old prefect badge, dad's tie, mum's glasses, a used condom everybody denied owning. One night I couldn't sleep, I went downstairs to get a drink and from the hallway I could hear this horrific squeaking."

"And...?"

"It was like a sound you'd hear in a nightmare coming from the kitchen. I went in to find a mouse had been caught, bleeding from the neck down in an attempt to wrench free. There were spots of blood on the trap. It was such a tiny thing, I felt sorry for it then."

"You wanted it that way though."

"Strange, I know. I'd set that particular trap, made it look like a small mouse bed. I hunkered down, picked it up while it yelped wildly."

"What did the kiss taste of?" Birdy asked.

"Despair and blood."

"Why did you kiss it?"

Jonno said, "How would you feel if you woke up to find you were dying painfully?"

From anyone else this confession would have appeared odd, but it was Jonno after all. In the distance, Jonno's mouse and the sperm from the condom that night fornicated to bear creatures resistant to traps and the mutant limbs of being caught off-guard.

Birdy used Photoshop to create a thumbnail image of herself. She liked this particular picture; she was wearing her mother's face and her grandmother's too. They'd sat on her skin like a moving canvass to dimple with white hot breaths from beyond. She had on her blue vest with the skull design. Her braided hair fell to her shoulders and you could make out the tattoo of a bracelet with a lizard's eye on her wrist. In the photo, her braids obscured part of her face. There were liquorice coloured buttons in clusters on her top, each button a full stop from a different conversation held in the day. Jonno had taken the picture. She wondered if through the lens, he saw not her but a projection of what he wanted her to be, only to print it and discover he was stuck with the version he had.

Birdy squinted at the image, trying to recall what she'd talked about that day and with whom but her memory had been scooped out of her pumpkin head. She could only remember a vague sense of vulnerability that had different coats in the seasons, her voice clinging to the flimsy threads of fragile things.

At first the thumbnail image invaded her life in harmless but intrusive ways. Bobbing across her orange laptop screen background in short sprints from one end to another, jammed in the CD slot, buried in her grey bucket of rice as though caught in an avalanche. She discovered it stuck on her kitchen notice board among the Jimmy Hendrix shark, the sloth private investigator and the baby weight lifter. Birdy couldn't recall placing any of them there. Why would she? It was weird; she didn't consider herself narcissistic enough to need the validation of seeing her image reflected in everything around her. What was next? The photo in her sandwiches? Swallowing them with a singular determination?

She and Jonno indulged in smoking some pretty strong skunk every so often and she always felt high and malleable afterwards. Her memory was lousy now. She'd told Jonno so the other day; her memory felt like eels slipping through her fingers.

Birdy worked for an arts organisation in Lewisham. The company programmed everything from theatre, to comedy, to spoken word and secret cinema screenings. They had a big, open loft office with wooden beams and windows in the ceiling that allowed wailing flashes of light to seep through. There was a storeroom cupboard at the back with old computers, flyers, branded items, CDs and anything you could label miscellaneous. Birdy was a National Coordinator, she met with artists and oversaw the running of the programme.

She deeply resented working in an open plan environment. There was no privacy. People saw your successes but they watched for your weaknesses too. Their eyes were pockets collecting every flaw. The director Martin was usually dressed in his favourite attire of jeans and T-shirts except when he had important meetings with potential partners. That was the arts; people went for that carefully conceived casual nonchalance with their appearance. If they wanted to crank it up a notch, they'd be quirkily casually dressed. Never flashy, which would be cheap. More often than not, arts practitioners were white middle-class. Birdy thought she could identify them in a crowd thanks to the privilege they wore almost indifferently and an understated cool. They were birds with purple breasts.

By twelve o'clock that afternoon Birdy was bored of wading through emails from artists enquiring about opportunities and a report she was only half-heartedly writing. She took a break by rifling through the store cupboard on the hunt for an old flyer. The store room had a red door; this always amused Birdy, as though it led to another dimension. It was full of boxes and files and needed a good clear out. Sometimes, you could hear the conversations of the staff from the women's shelter that floated just beyond their reach and a horizon covered in bruises. She heard the door shut quietly and turned to see Martin behind her.

"How's it going?" he asked.

"Surreptitious." Birdy dropped the box of flyers she'd been holding, the patient paper cuts sighed disappointedly.

"What?"

"Surreptitious, word of the day."

"Oh! Your word of the day thing, not sure what it means. Listen, this is awkward, so I'm going to jump right in." He leaned back against the wooden shelf. "You're a very attractive young woman, even more so since you've grown in confidence these last few years and I'm flattered, I really am, but you should stop."

Birdy looked at him confusingly, her expression wrinkled.

"I don't understand."

"Stop sending pictures of yourself to my home. Karen found

them and she's very upset. She thinks I'm having an affair with you, it's causing me a lot of stress at home right now."

Birdy's face flushed, her armpits tingled with sweat.

"Martin, I don't know what you're talking about. I didn't send any pictures." Although she said this with conviction, a nagging doubt buried itself in her chest. Had she sent pictures and forgotten? Surely she'd remember doing something so stupid? She'd never felt any form of attraction to Martin, only gratitude. He'd been a mentor to her. A lump formed in her throat, a prism with a miniature version of her trapped inside trying to smash through.

"What sort of pictures?" she asked. "Show me."

"Well, it's the same one, only different sizes. Hold on." He stuck his hand into his back pocket, pulled it out and dropped it in her palm. It was a strip of passport sized images, the same one she'd been spotting in incongruous places around her flat. It felt hot on her palm, a paper runway. She saw the remnants of her career in LEGO sized cases, lugging themselves up that runway with no flight at the end to catch.

"I recognise the picture, but I didn't send it. I'm sorry for any trouble this has caused; please tell your wife that."

Martin rubbed his face. "Okay, I'm confused. You've been acting a little strange lately, distracted and agitated. If something's going on, you can come to me."

"Thanks," she weakly said.

Martin walked out, leaving the door slightly ajar. Birdy's skin mottled with embarrassment. She couldn't trust herself anymore. What she did and didn't do, what she saw and didn't see. It had all become one blurry gulf she was feeling her way around. She wondered if other members of staff knew. She opened the door a little wider and several people were staring at their screens with a little too much intent. She glanced at the window in the ceiling and tongues were wagging against the glass, or maybe it was rain. The other workers were becoming animals at her expense, laughing at her. Dinosaur jaws sprang from their backs, hyena heads jutted from their stomachs. Their hands became horse hooves pointing. Birdy shrank back, but before she knew it she was on the ceiling, hanging from her paranoia as though it was a rope and she a circus act.

Jonno was a thief. He stole the gleam from people's eyes and used them as half-stars on his tongue, a starry pink entity that required damaged light. It flicked over her hard nipples and concave chest, it traced the outlines of new lies that sprang out of her skin like small, wet cellophane bags.

Jonno had been adopted. It accounted for his sense of displacement. His parents told him during a furious row about money. It made sense at the time; there had always been a niggling doubt. The ghost showed its head, its blotchy skin. It wriggled between them and used its mouth to pick up the rest of its body parts. Jonno had been pleased to find out. He said that his house was so miserable, even the furniture didn't look happy to be there.

They met at a Roots Manuva gig. Jonno was impressed by the way she pretended to be a member of the press who'd had her ID stolen. She conned her way backstage, reminding him of a frenetic drum beat that gathered speed and rhythm. The beat lodged in his throat until he couldn't swallow anymore.

Jonno looked like Lenny Kravitz, something he got fed up of being told. He had that one slack, smaller eye that seemed to be elsewhere while simultaneously having a conversation with you. It was a black marble crawling under your skin, floating in someone's glass of Guinness blinking away the creamy foam or stuck to a shiny copper two pence piece in your wallet, like a tiny fallen planet. He spoke in a calm, measured way. Birdy had been intrigued by the things left unsaid.

They fed on a diet of kaleidoscopes those first few months. They rocked each other in tight embraces at smoky, intimate music gigs, watched obscure films in kitsch, independent cinemas, had sex in the dressing room of a Sense charity shop between items of clothing, partied at the temporary homes of squatters who didn't have last names and smoked everything but their nomadic sensibilities. They streaked through Victoria Park at night with nothing but the winter chill turning their limbs into the body parts of store dummies. One dead arm, one dead leg, kisses at body temperature. When they went night swimming, the pale moonlight was anaemic. They watched it swallow headlights from the cars on the motorway in the distance. Jonno looked like a beautiful, black shark in the water, a fin in his back, leaning to the right like a silvery right angle triangle. He came up for air and the water rushed off his skin, flashed his sharp, white teeth. He held her, handed her the shark smile as she wore his fin. Afterwards, he told her there was a beauty in destruction.

The thumbnails grew bolder with each appearance. One day, during lunch at work when the office was empty, they filled the seats, becoming larger and larger until they obliterated the Mac screens. They appeared on the work noticeboard, faces scribbled out by marker pens, on the desks and in the drawers of her colleagues, who took her to one side asking why she was circulating pictures of herself. They sat beside her on train rides home trying to communicate to her, dark eyes small, haunted reflections she tried to block out. She became obsessed with trying to find the original among them; perhaps if she could identify it, get rid of it, she'd somehow root them all out.

She couldn't fuck Jonno properly for a while because the thumbnails keep clambering into bed with them, mimicking the sounds of her climaxing until she couldn't tell where she began and they ended.

On an afternoon during her company's quarterly roundtable, Birdy stood by the large flip chart for her ten-minute presentation on regional developments and potential projects with new and existing partners. She could hear the thumbnails under the murmurs of her curious colleagues, a quiet rustling, rumbling in the distance. Her colleagues tilted their faces up expectantly. Birdy's mind went blank; her hand trembled erratically, trying to silence her thumbnails with the blue marker pen. She gazed past everyone as if hypnotised, held by some force. The thumbnails, hundreds of them, were tumbling through the open skylight onto Birdy's desk, like a waterfall of images executing their perfect landing.

After a half hour break, the team came back to discover Birdy's desk on fire; crackling and snapping as objects melted and smoke filled the air. The fire brigade was called. The team waited downstairs in the café anxiously. Birdy sat on a table by herself trying not to cry. Martin, red-faced, scowled at her from across the room.

The thumbnails accosted Birdy in the hallway of her flat. The muddy river in the ceiling from the leak in the bathroom above had instructed them too. Birdy imagined the pull of the tide occupying hiding places. She wondered then about the watermarks she'd missed spotting. She'd have to leave in a few months before the water submerged the flat. All watermarks formed a dangerous alliance, however small. The thumbnails now were thin, hollow-eyed. Tufts of hair pulled from their heads. Crusts of dried blood surrounded their nostrils like dormant red bulbs. Two front teeth were missing from each one, as if they'd taken a wrong exit and some cruel beast had ravaged them, collecting parts like souvenirs. They watched her change in the bedroom, followed her around whispering, "Birdy, do you remember the first time?"

Of course she did. She flew inside herself when the needle hit the snake in her arm, greedy green veins that grew fatter. She flew from her centre in a dizzying ride with no ceiling or floor erected as boundaries. She flew above the houses and appeared as a dot on Google Maps. While she travelled, she caught bits of conversations between the night sky and the ground with a sweaty palm. The rush of blood to the head, the distorted light Birdy had eaten from to feel bigger. Each time she took a bite she grew.

She yelled, "See? I can be bigger! I don't have to feel like I'm looking at the world from knee-level anymore. It can look up at me! I don't have to be small."

But when the thumbnails began to appear, they were disgruntled. They floated in inappropriate places in case there was a chance of rain. They called to the tide. They flew at Birdy in her dreams, arms outstretched and dead-eyed. They opened their mouths and she slid in. There she exploded like a bomb and the bits of her body never reassembled.

Birdy curled into a foetal position on the grey lino kitchen floor. Some of the thumbnails had impaled themselves on cutlery that had thinned into needles. She noticed then that their faces had withered even more. She began to cry. She lay there looking up at that first time as if shrouded in a dirty cloud. When she came down she'd slumped into Jonno's arms. He stroked her hair, kissed her forehead. The kiss grew gnarled fingers. Through their drug-fuelled haze she saw Jonno the magician holding a small bag of white powder.

"Baby," he said. "Let me show you this trick: bag of coke, now you see it, now you don't."

She picked up after six rings. "Hello?"

"I've been calling your mobile. What's going on?" Jonno's voice was deep, croaky and sleep-lined.

"Martin gave me a warning, he threatened to fire me! I can't lose my job!"

"Shh, Birdy, calm the fuck down, they can't sack you just like that. There are procedures they have to follow, there's probably a disciplinary action first. What did you tell him?"

"Don't worry, he doesn't know you're a biochemist or about your hideous tempering with my body. I don't know what's going on; I'm having bad reactions to these experiments of yours. What are you putting in these cocktails we tried? I'm not right anymore, it's messing with my wiring or something!"

"Birdy, shut up, not on the phone. You want to walk to the police station and make an announcement? Listen to me, relax. You're not helping yourself by panicking."

"Martin said he got pictures."

"What pictures?"

"The last ones you took of me, someone sent them to his house, his wife found them."

Silence, then the line crackled, the echoes of something lost. Jonno said, "I'm coming over" and the line clicked off. Birdy still held the handset. Only she stood at the end of Jonno's mouth, looking down on its curved line as though it was a well to drink from. And the phone would be a useful instrument, she just hadn't figured out how.

Birdy remembered then that she and Jonno had argued about Martin while he was taking the pictures.

"I don't like the way he looks at you with a kind of longing."
Click.

"You're being ridiculous, he's my boss. He gave me a job."
Click.

"Yeah, and now he wants to collect. I know how men think, OK? I know how I'd think. You can't see it." *Click.*

"Come on, he's been like a father to me." *Click.*

"You're so idiotically naïve sometimes, Birdy. He didn't like me on sight." *Click.*

"You didn't like him either, you're so paranoid." *Click.*

"Yeah, I'm paranoid. Keep your distance, I don't trust him." *Click, click, click!*

Suddenly she saw Jonno with all the faces he wore, the mystery in him that had trapped a curious boat, a one-winged plane and wrong footed other means of transport. Ever since Jonno had arrived in her life things had happened. The dull, fevered ache that kept getting hungry, the pattern in the sky with six tentacles that followed her everywhere, the timer on her heart she couldn't shake off. Her pillow was made of blades, not feathers. A boomerang in the air became an elbow looking for a body. She recalled the looks of contempt he'd shot her, sandwiched between strokes and conversations. The smoke-rimmed kisses he left down her stomach designed to call flames to set her alight. Jonno's addiction to damaging people, the beauty he saw in destruction. She wondered what she'd done with all these signs. Had she deliberately shoved them in a drawer to gather dust?

She was drunk with knowledge. Cruelty was a currency in relationships. She couldn't feel her face; she touched it tentatively as if trying to familiarise herself with the lines and angles. Two of her front teeth fell out. *Oh, God.* She ran to the bathroom mirror. She couldn't escape herself there. She looked gaunt, sickly. She pulled her hair back, a handful of braids fell out, dropping into the sink leaving a bald patch. The light in her eyes had gone. She turned the tap on, the fat black braids slid down, she looked into the darkness of the plughole struggling to breathe, trying to see something she could hold on to. She ran through the flat turning all the taps on, watching the water spill. She searched the floor for her teeth. She couldn't find them.

She heard Jonno coming up the stairs leading to her apartment. He had a key. She opened the kitchen window. The remaining thumbnails leaped out, her two discoloured teeth gleaming in their mouths. She knew Jonno commanded them with every step. The front door lock turned. Her spine caved. Outside, the thumbnails, those lost fragments of herself flew past the metal gods pretending to be lampposts. Maybe they were headed to the roots of trees for second lives, or maybe to the tide.

The Arrangement of Skin

The crows emerged wet with saliva. Each sported one blue eye. In the garden, they congregated near the washing line as though it was their tightrope, a tenuous line of breath.

Carolina watched from her kitchen window. They flew at her face, as if she were salvation in a glass house. She checked the garden door was locked, that the sleep marks on her arms hadn't migrated to her face. She busied herself making a sandwich. Muffled sounds from the basement seemed like a distant thing. Carolina loved her basement, it craved the things she did. Broken wrists, spines she attempted to re-grow in maroon plant pots, sour pink tongues. Her basement understood wanting to be filled with things beyond comprehension, like a thousand injured women queuing inside you and tiny breakable houses.

Carolina lived in Clapham, in a Victorian house with a black slate roof that was nestled behind some shrubbery on a quiet street. It was decorated in muted cream tones but the plum sofa, Moroccan throw rugs and bright lava lamps rebelled. Her kitchen had a large farmhouse table, a black Victorian style stove and some cast iron pots hanging on the wall. Upstairs, the smaller second bedroom held an old, empty wooden cot. The window was half open. Street symphonies of squealing tires, clicking heels and loud voices filtered through.

Carolina finished off her sandwich with relish. She was a heavyset woman with a permanently weathered expression and thick whitish-blonde hair. She knew lots of the answers on *Who Wants to Be a Millionaire* and whiled away her evenings listening to LBC radio station well into the night, blue eyes intermittently becoming grey.

Halloween arrived, the time of year those little visitors came to her door. She always ensured she had a selection of sweets and chocolates, the house was warm and the scent of baked apple pie lingered. She always prepared her coins in anticipation.

Around 8pm, nine-year-old Otto's skeleton costume caught on the rusted spike of a gate, causing a tear in one trouser leg. He lagged behind to inspect the damage while his pack of friends rushed ahead. He heard their squeals of excitement just ahead of him, around the corner. A couple of doors after his accident, he lifted Carolina's lion door knocker and asked if his friends had stopped by already. She said, "No, but I can help you with that, dear," pointing at his torn costume. Her smile was welcoming, her eyes kind. He took off his mask; it was rude to talk to someone with your face covered up. His brown curls sprang free.

He stepped into the hallway, leaving his perforated guardian angel as she lay, bleeding on the pavement. Inside, Otto missed the children's faces pressed against the glass of the clock, a different face for each step; their breaths small ice storms. She gave Otto money. They chatted for a few minutes; he laughed and ate three cubes of Belgian chocolate. She prepared the sweetest cup of warm milk. He took large gulps. It tasted delicious. After a few minutes, he felt light-headed. The living room began to swim. He slipped off the sofa. The last thing he saw was Carolina standing over him, watching his face curiously.

Carolina decided to make a chicken sandwich for her guest. Living alone in winter was particularly lonely. It was nice to have company. Earlier in the day, the EDF energy man came to read the meter. He waffled on about new meters and the length of time it would take to visit properties in the area. Eventually he left, a jacket grey moving through her doorway. The microfibers travelled through the air, down her throat and into an asphalt road that bent to a different time, to the iron lake that showed Carolina's reflection aged twelve. And Villa Holm, Småland, Sweden. A home, mausoleum and witness with its undulating green grounds and large, decadent rooms, making prisoners of them all. Then, Carolina liked to fish, talking while they dangled on hooks, dripping translucent rays on her feet.

At dinner she'd slam her prize in the middle of the table before her father Olan. She'd wait for a reaction but his eyes flickered over it dismissively.

"Carolina, pass the butter," he'd instructed coldly.

Sometimes her spoils were dead squirrels, an Ostrich egg, a man she'd met in the town centre whom Olan had politely escorted out. Olan was remote; his face serious with wire-rimmed spectacles and a furrowed expression. A psychologist, he lost himself in his work. Their quiet dinners were often interrupted by violent screams from a room above. They came from her mother Agneta, the one from whom Carolina had never experienced any real affection or mothering. She knew Agneta had had several breakdowns and she appeared to Carolina to carry the shattered bits of her life with slender, tapered fingers. Once Carolina caught their old housekeeper sniggering on the phone to someone, saying, "A psychologist with his mad wife and weird child, can you imagine?"

Agneta was a fragile, beautiful, waif-like woman. She seemed incapable of existing without assistance yet she was deceptively physically strong. On one occasion, she smashed plates up and down their staircase, screaming throughout, rushed at Olan wielding an old hunting knife while he entertained guests, demanding to be freed from her confinement. She cut her stomach before the shocked guests who looked at Olan with pity, confusion and disdain. Crawling on the floor, gripped by some terrible pain, she claimed Jesus had visited her. Olan had to drag her from the room. Arms flailing, Agneta hollered that she would take bites out of all the guests before they left. The guests looked on in horror, ashen-faced and embarrassed, although whether it was for themselves, the psychologist or his mad wife, was never quite clear.

Some days Agneta cried relentlessly, hollering in her room, turning it upside down searching for an amulet she said Jesus had left her. She watched her daughter suspiciously. When Carolina slept, she felt Agneta slipping into her head, planting images of bloody soil, broken limbs and battered faces.

Carolina couldn't recall exactly when it began. But she remembered watching bread rise in the oven thinking it looked like skin. She saw blood vessels in the loaf exploding like tiny, runny planets. That same evening, she spotted her father's study door open, light flooding the cold hallway. She entered and walked up to Olan who stood by the French windows looking out into the grounds and further still into the woods. A creature on all fours with pale, moonlight hair darted between the trees. It was Agneta. Father and daughter stood rooted to the spot connected by something they dared not define. They knew this had been coming. Agneta had refused to come back into the house for three days and was now completely feral. Tired and weary from years of suffering, Olan made no move to retrieve his wife.

They watched the lake darkening and stayed until the night swallowed Agneta whole.

Carolina carried the sandwich to the basement door on a rose patterned tray. The muffled sounds became louder. She set the tray down and unlocked the door. Otto's face in the crack of light was pale, sweaty as though he'd been wrestling with something.

"Please," he said, voice breaking, eyes glimmering darkly, "Let me be your apprentice… I can learn from you."

Agneta stood behind him silvery and snarling, clutching her stone amulet. Carolina shoved Otto backwards, shaken by a reminder of her future, watching him tumble down the stairs. Her mouth curled. She counted to ten before retreating into the kitchen. The clock read 5pm. *Deal or no Deal* would be starting soon. The thought of having an apprentice excited her. She began to think of all the things she could teach him. She opened the window so that later the glassy-eyed crows Agneta sent could return to her womb for their nightly death.

Snapper

I'm scooping up a broken map of fish bones from my soup when you say, "It's great honestly, you should see the craftsmanship on this thing! And God knows how old it is."

We're sitting in Lazzaria restaurant, complete with dim lighting, cabaret style setting, deep red velvet curtains and oddly-shaped nooks. Renaissance art fills the walls, ornate chandeliers dangle from pristine white ceilings and exotic scents linger in the air. It feels as though we're in a play. Our supporting cast of diners are found objects who stumble onto set randomly. The sound of cutlery clinking against plates is surprisingly comforting. The opera singer is the only guest star; she seems to be simultaneously singing at several tables as if she's on wheels. Her voice carries into people's meals. A daffodil in her hair grows from being watered by wine, elderflower and gin.

I say, "A samurai sword as a gift? Isn't that a weird thing for a client to do?"

"Nah, it's a nice gesture." You break a piece of herb bread from the deep violet bowl in the middle of the table. "He was just trying to show appreciation."

"Are you legally allowed to possess it?" I ask. "I mean, it's a weapon."

"I don't know, Perry Mason." You chuckle a little. "But I'm keeping it."

You finish the bread with relish, crumbs spilling into your

lap. There is a stain on your crisp, blue shirt from a piece of tomato shaped like a tear. The sight makes me smile. I like that you're not quite polished. I imagine you at school as the kid whose shirt was never tucked in properly, whose shoelaces frequently came undone. I picture teachers liking you despite themselves. In my mind's eye, you are holding a white piece of chalk from your youth, drawing outlines around our snapshots that will be eroded by the weather. I watch you, recalling the memory of our first meeting.

I was holding a bag of oxtail on Green Street at Upton Park when the accident happened. It was evening and the throngs from the market had vanished, most stalls packed up. Only a few people were ambling around here and there. My newly braided hair was tight on my scalp. Just as the cars collided, I felt a headache coming. Nearby, a man was leaning against the window of the closed Percy Ingle bakery smoking a cigarette and a woman was putting tights on in the phone box up ahead. I wondered then if we all felt the sound of the crash reverberate through us simultaneously as a black Mercedes careened into a Blue Honda Civic making a U-turn. The Honda Civic tossed in the air, before crashing against the boulder on the side and then landing upside down. Exhaust pipe smoke curled in the air, a silent signal calling to passing ignitions.

I watched the scene with other onlookers who appeared from nowhere and were waiting for somebody else to jump into action. The door of the Civic opened and you fell to the ground, hurling yourself up slowly, limping. I assessed you quickly; black male, late twenties, lean, attractive.

You walked towards me and shouted in my direction, "Hey! Call a fucking ambulance. My boys are in there, two of them aren't moving." Your voice was rough, urgent. There was an unapologetic ruggedness about you. Your left arm was bloody. There were shards of glass in your left hand and on your hair like crystals. The heat off your body was palpable.

"Lady, please call an ambulance!"

You were getting closer, right in my personal space, which jolted me into action. The bag of oxtail meat dropped. I steered you to a seat that had been left by a stall area. I fished my phone out of my handbag and called 999. I closed the flap of my phone, dropping it inside my bag just as the woman from the phone box stumbled out. Drunk, she had left her heels inside.

"The ambulance is coming. Good luck," I said awkwardly, stepping away.

"Stay with me," you begged, placing your hand on the small of my back, leaving it there.

I felt its heat, its quiet anxiety. I was surprised by your gesture, by the intimacy of it.

Afterwards, I could hardly contain my excitement, my curiosity. Something in me had a chemical reaction to you. I held the scrap of paper with your number in my hand, sullied at the edges from a pen that had leaked in my pocket. I called you two days after the accident. Fuck protocol. I offered to cook you oxtail stew. You laughed, charmed.

I phoned my cousin Inez several weeks later to tell her I met a man from an accident. I worried something had dislodged in the both of us the night of the crash which I had traced and tried to reinsert into an opening in your skin when your guard was down, when you were breathing against my nipple. I told her I feared that one day you would leave me in search of other accidents that are grave, life threatening, with pretty women on the periphery waiting to mop up blood with their mouths, to carry debris in small handbags they will need later. How could I compete with that?

I explained we watched footage of car crashes as research for your games design work. Your eyes were inexplicably bright, alert, as if you were nostalgic for the tyres screeching and the sound of metal crushing, for a vehicle being tossed in the air. When we were watching, you ran your fingers over my knees, turned the volume up as a crash exploded in our ears. Inez harrumphed at the other end of the line, clearly disapproving. I told her you were traumatised. You were showing initiative and emotional intelligence by confronting your trauma so boldly.

"What about the guy who works at the council?" Inez replied. "Dave somebody or other, he was nice. What happened to him?"

"He was nice," I answered, annoyed at the way she always seems to like the men I date after they've left my life. I pictured her bird hands holding the receiver, her elegant neck, her confused expression.

I put the phone down irritated, regretting the call. I walked to my bedroom closet, found the clothes you were wearing on the night of the accident I had sneaked from your flat; a pair of blue jeans and a black T-shirt. I tried them on in the mirror and sat for a while, listening for a piece of small crushed metal spinning inside me, expanding with every breath. I closed my eyes and saw you coming at me with your teeth bared and arm bloodied. The cars were wrecked behind you, smoke in the air. Caught by surprise, I watched your mouth moving, picturing your internal injuries. I thought, *Yes, this is a man who needs me.* I became moist remembering this scene. I pulled my panties down, masturbating on the bedroom floor in the glare of afternoon sunlight.

After dinner, we walk along the Southbank hand in hand. Ripples of the murky water call to lost objects. We build a boat from a swiped menu and let it sail in the city, listing the number of things it will crash into.

Several days later, you cut your hand with the sword. Worried, I rush over. Your flat has a rustic charm that always relaxes me, all wooden floors and earth-toned furnishings. While you tell me about the latest video game you're designing, I lick the blood slipping into your palm lines. You've just cut your hair in a style from the nineties and could be an extra member of a Tribe Called Quest. We make love in your rumpled bed with the damaged, purple headboard that rattles. I watch the angle of your arm leaning against the wall, a half-bow in my intoxicated gaze. Your mouth opens over the pulse in my neck as if it will run away. I kiss your shoulder, tasting a corner of promise.

Later, I hold the samurai sword. It's heavier than I expected, with a long blade and a dragon's mouth on the black handle.

I notice the change slowly. Over the following weeks, you become obsessed with samurai films; *Goyokin*, *Chushingura*, *Ghost Dog*, *Way of the Samurai*, *Throne of Blood*, *13 Assassins*, *Yojimbo*, *Harakiri*, *Seven Samurai*, the same way you were addicted to watching car crashes. You watch these films entranced. We sit through a couple together. I move restlessly, picking at threads I don't quite understand. You begin to train in your basement, surrounded by the clutter of ordinary things; boxing gloves, old B-movie posters acting as a happy audience, a broken record player with a needle scratching the sky. Copper pipes in the ceiling hiss as you practice, darting and lunging at an invisible sparring partner that becomes an enemy in commencing days. Once or twice at lunch, you use the sword to carve roast beef as though it's perfectly normal. On one such occasion, I notice the gleam in your eye becoming a tiny silhouette. *Cut, cut, cut.*

You are laughing about a comedy sketch you saw on Channel 4, rubbing the sword against a large kitchen utensil, sharpening your instrument. The smell of oxtail gravy makes my mouth water. And the rattling in my head begins.

In early April, while we're curled up on the sofa one evening, you tell me you've been fired from your job. You don't explain the circumstances fully, except to say you dangled one of the directors out of the window for insulting you. You are defiant, dismissive even. "Luna, fuck them! I worked there for seven years and that's how I get treated? All the directors are on cocaine anyway. I'll start my own company."

The concern on my face stops you in your stride. You place your hand gently on my back, steadying the anxiety gathering.

"Baby, don't look so scared. This is what happens when the time comes."

I grab your hands, holding onto their warmth. "When what time comes, Cosmo?"

"There are wars looming, enemies hovering. People take their level of comfort for granted in this country, nobody's prepared."

I shake my head slowly. "You're talking in riddles, I don't understand."

We continue watching TV. An early episode of *Twin Peaks* is on. Setting your half-drunk can of Guinness down, you uncurl like a snake ready to dispatch poison. "You understand, I know you do." I can feel the intensity of your gaze when you add, "I need you to be on my side, for both our sakes."

I'm vaguely aware of the door opening, your footsteps towards the kitchen and the samurai sword next to the bowl of fruit there. I'm wrestling with the idea of telling you that lately, I am thirsty all the time, so parched I could drain a whole house of half its water supply.

At that point, I notice the paper ship we built from the restaurant menu in the doorway. It's worn, dirty around the edges from its travels. The words of the menu have changed. It nudges its way in, on a path of murky water.

We're looking through photos of our trip to Venice last year when you tell me about the hospital. The paper ship loiters in the background, attempting to gain entrance into the images. A dog barks in the distance, pizza boxes are piled on the floor next to the bed and the scent of pepperoni is still strong.

You were standing outside the hospital, blown onto the steps by a whistle that became a wind. Cold, you peered into people's faces to identify their sickness, wanting to cross the busy reception and take the lift up to the wards. Only, it didn't feel like it could be a mere few minutes' walk. It felt like a journey, in which you imagined losing your hands to confectionary machines that dispatch stolen hands for 70p, £1.50, £2.30. You saw yourself confronting increasingly docile versions of your face when the lift doors open at each floor. People on the steps began to whistle. A nurse standing by a window knocked on the glass looking straight at you. But you walked away trembling, grabbing roots in your pockets to steady yourself.

I don't know what to say to this story. I go over several responses in my mind but none of them feels right.

Jesus, that's a strange tale.

Why would you go to the hospital?

Do you think there was some sort of epidemic being transferred by compulsive urges to whistle?

I stop myself because I'd be accommodating whatever this was, whatever we aren't identifying by saying any of those things.

You turn to me suddenly, taking a deep drag of your

cigarette. "Don't you ever want to be reborn? Don't you want to know what it feels like?"

The cigarette's amber tip brightens then simmers. I can hear the leaking shower in the bathroom dripping, filling my eardrums. "Sometimes, Cosmo," I say. "I think we have common grounds because of our mutual self-loathing."

You fold me into your arms then. "Luna, Luna, Luna." You chant my name softly, as though an open window has taken a breath. Your mouth hovers over my eye lovingly at first and then as if contemplating swallowing my vision.

Several days later, while looking for some aspirin, I find your work dismissal letter tucked away in the sock drawer, dated six months earlier than the date you gave me.

One blustery evening, we're lounging around the flat. We smoke weed, drink shots of rum. Sade croons on the CD player. I leaf through a copy of *Time* magazine. You're playing some Playstation game intensely as I doze off on the sofa.

When I come round, you're standing over me naked, holding the samurai sword covered in blood. Your hands are trembling; you're breathing heavily, your penis is flaccid.

I stumble up in awkward movements, pat myself down for injuries, brain scrambling, but it's not my blood.

"Cosmo, what's going on? What have you done?" I ask, voice a whisper. Touching my shoulder, you edge forward gingerly as if I'm a mirage. Your eyes are wild. "In the game, baby, I had to kill the man at the bridge to get the keys, see? He wouldn't let me have keys to the kingdom otherwise."

"What the fuck are you talking about?" I yell. "Oh my God! Tell me what's going on, Cosmo, what have you done?"

My head spins. The wooden floor is covered in blood. Panic inside me rises.

"You're such a bitch! Why can't you ever be on my side?" you scream. You start to babble about the stupid game, about being a general in Japan during a past incarnation, about members of your army waiting to meet you, ready to overthrow the British government. You continue rambling while I'm darting around the flat, checking the bedroom, the kitchen and the bathroom. But there is no body and the paper ship is battered, covered in blood. I hear the front door click. You are gone, out in the night, naked and waving your samurai sword.

I throw my trainers on, bolting after you. Only in a vest and bottoms, the air is cool on my skin. You're too quick, already rounding the corner and heading into the high street.

"Cosmo, wait!" My voice is strangled. You don't turn around. I take deep breaths. The high street is busy. I pass a Seven Eleven feeling parched, its neon glow seeps into the whites of my eyes. My throat becomes a small dessert. *I could drink half that store*, I think. It's urgent, pressing. I notice a woman pushing a baby in a pram holding a bottle. I snatch the bottle from the baby's hands.

"Hey!" the woman barks. "What do you think you're doing?"

I ignore her, unscrewing the cap and gulping warm milk down. It spills on my chin as I try to keep you in my sights. You are weaving through the road, people stop to stare, car horns blare. We are pressed against dark corners shaped like pockets. Sirens screaming in my ears look for other entry points into our bodies. The gulf between us grows, cracked and dry. I attempt to moisten it with my milky tongue. I think of our timelines being caught in bicycle wheels, of our love being born from an accident, of you being drawn back to the traffic, spilling crumbs into your laugh. I remember my snapper meal from the restaurant months back then.

Like you, it snapped at the end of a line before landing into stillness forever.

My legs begin to burn. Smoke in my nostrils gathers as if I've set myself alight internally. I can see you holding the sword up, talking to a God growing in your peripheral vision. I keep going for our sake, but we are changing beneath flickering city lights, a malleable sky. The tip of the sword is our compass. We are breakable things running. And I am waiting to trip, fall and catch some semblance of you I recognise.

Jody

I'm standing in the cash point queue on Deptford High Street when the guy at the machine turns to me and says, "I hate finding out my balance, don't you? In fact, I don't want to know today." He presses the screen option for cash without balance and throws me a warm, ruddy-faced smile over his shoulder.

"I know what you mean," I answer, trying not to let the surprise show on my face. People from London don't talk to each other in cash point queues. The man looks like Will Self, all feral, gleaming blue eyes and striking features, as if he's just crawled out of moist soil naked, fully-formed, baring his unevenly shaped teeth in daylight, dusted off and thrown on the first pieces of clothing he could get his hands on.

"Yeah, it's always less money than you think it is." My luggage, although not a large amount turns out to be somewhat of a hindrance; a plastic bag full of charity shop items with a broken handle I bunched at the top, a handbag containing way too much shit, a rucksack that keeps slipping off my shoulders.

It's market day in Deptford, which means the smell of fish in the air, zigzagging through throngs of people would be more awkward than usual and potentially knocking into the coppery spare parts of stalls. The man stuffs notes in his pocket, moves away from the stunted line. He has an erratic, restless energy that would be jarring in an uprooted white room, a tub full of mauve paint, your mother's dinner table. On Deptford High Street, he fits right in.

At the machine, I prop up the plastic bag with my knee, punching in my pin as quickly as my numb fingers will allow. I spot him lingering on the side, leaning into his steps, trying to be more certain of something. He's almost in the road at this point, almost in the windscreen of the battered Peugeot 406 stuttering round the curve. His blue windbreaker billows. I can't tell if his corduroys are black or a really dark grey. He's skinny. His bulbous head of thinning brown hair makes me think of an onion peeling in the cold, his head shedding layers that fall into spaces between silences, shoeprints, mouths of squirrels in the green church grounds, repeatedly eating it as a daily bread.

"What's your name? What do you do?" he asks. There's slow curiosity and wonder in his face, as though he's looking at me yet seeing something else. Maybe my rainbow-coloured gills are trying to pierce through an inadequate, checked coat, whispering against the lining, craving water, light, thin surfaces. The gills are a little damp under my buttoned black cardigan and I can still taste a slither of salty sea water beneath my tongue.

"My name's Opal." I pull the bank card from the slot, slip it into my handbag. "I do a bit of this and that."

"Opal! Beautiful name, old-fashioned somehow. Would you like to come for a drink?" he asks. I can't quite place his accent but he sounds as if he grew up on a farm somewhere, riding tractors that doubled as sturdy accomplices under moonlight, chasing versions of himself from the pig pen.

A couple of women in the queue eye us, unable to hide their disdain at his unkempt appearance. His large hands tremble a little, a patch of red crawls up the exposed skin of his throat. My friend wouldn't be meeting me for a few hours. Between killing time with a stranger or wandering the cold streets in search of somewhere to vegetate, time with a stranger seems like the better option. Either he didn't get the hint earlier that I wanted to be left alone or he didn't care either way. His lopsided grin looks downright shifty at this point. There's something about the judgement oozing from the pores of the women in the queue that rankles. My gills begin to whimper. My mouth turns dry. The hopefulness in his expression kills my last reservation.

"Sure, why not?" I say, grabbing my bag firmly, checking behind to ensure I hadn't dropped anything.

We cross the street in a rush of movement, wind and unexpected crackling energy. It's freezing. I'm so cold, I barely break step when I see a rastaman in a green flannel shirt with his arm around a silver fish almost as big as he is, a charity shop worker pricing his assistant up at £10 in the window, a train set at full steam bursting through the stomach of an inflatable woman by the basket at the pound shop entrance. We're on the side of the station as translucent scales fall from my eyes. He misses this.

"What's your name? Where are you from?" I ask, trying to shake bits of seaweed from my head.

"I'm Jody with a y," he answers, catching a breeze in his mouth. "I'm from Shropshire, it's beautiful. Not like here! I tell you, I've been here twelve months and still can't get used to it. The people need to fucking relax." He sticks his hand out. I shake it, wondering if he can feel the lines in my palm becoming thin threads. I hoist the rucksack further up my shoulder knowing if it were to fall and spill open, he'd be surprised by its contents, by the things that could be moulded, stuffed and talked into silence.

"So where are we going, Jody with a y?"

We pause momentarily outside some junk shop that sells everything, including flip-flops in winter and model double-decker buses. A grey cat slinks towards him. He bends down to stroke it.

"I love nature and animals, don't you? Impressive creatures."

He gives the cat one last rub for the road. It purrs, stretching.

We're on the move again when he finally answers, "I'm meeting my mate Donny in the pub. Salt of the earth, that guy! I tell you, he took me under his wing when I first got here. He's full of surprises. We're sitting on the train one day and he starts saying, 'fucking spades this' and 'spades that'! I'm shocked by this because we all bleed the same in my eyes. Do you know what I mean, Opal? Anyway, we're sitting in the pub one day and in walks his missus. I nearly fell off my chair! She's black like you. And I'm thinking, that fucker talking 'spades this', 'spades that,' all the while he's got a black missus. I tell you, I was dumbfounded!"

He waves his arm about, stops before a betting shop where a couple of guys are shifting about slowly, sullenly, almost disappearing into their coats before the bored cashier.

"Well, Jody, that is conflicting," I say ruefully, swallowing the salt in my throat. "People are complex creatures."

In the betting shop light, I notice the scar on his neck, a handmade bracelet sewn in.

"Good guy, though," he continues, bright and animated, beaming at me, yet looking ahead. "How old are you?" he asks.

I want to tell him I'm a hundred, two hundred, a newborn in borrowed limbs. Instead, I curl my lips up mysteriously. "Lead the way, Don Juan."

The pub is dingy, all depressing dark décor and animated white men watching football with beers in hand. There's a

Thai woman in a tight, corset-like top behind the bar. The large, dominating snooker table is surrounded. As I stash my stuff in a corner booth, I hear balls rolling into pockets.

A boy brandishing a snooker cue lunges at Jody. "What's she doing with you?" he says. "She's pretty." He laughs, darting from side to side.

Jody ruffles his hair playfully. "Get away, you little scamp!" He takes one last mock swipe at him before heading to the bar to order me a vodka and orange.

"Dad! You won't believe this!" The boy calls across the room. "Jody's got a girlfriend." He plonks himself in the stool beside me and then, as if he's been dialled down several notches, says shyly, "Hi, I'm Mason."

"Hi, Mason, I'm Opal. Did your dad teach you how to play snooker?" I glance up at the screen, still mystified by the level of emotion a game of grown men chasing a ball could evoke from other grown men. Mason nods, fishes a handful of sweets from his pocket and spreads them on the table. "Do you want one?"

"Thank you, darling." I lean forward, pick one in an orange wrapper and unwrap it before popping it into my mouth.

Jody and I are about ten minutes into our conversation when a handsome, dark-haired, bearded burly man in his mid-forties ambles over.

"Well, fuck me with a toothpick! Jody, she's a beauty. What on earth is she doing with you? Did you drug her to get her down here? Stop copy-catting yours truly by getting a black girlfriend."

"Fuck off!" Jody retorts, guffawing over his beer. "Am I ever, you and your 'spades this', 'spades that' only to have a black missus. You're wrong in the head."

The man slurs his words. "I'm Donny, sweetheart. You met

my boy Mason earlier. Don't listen to him." He angles his head at Jody. "He's a prick. Good heart, but a prick." He parks himself at the table, studying my features.

Simultaneously, I feel the gaze of other men, aware I must be somewhat of a rarity in a place like this. None of this fazes me though. I shrug my coat off, leaning into Donny's gaze.

"God, I wish I was twenty years younger looking at you," he remarks. He's rakish and the gleam in his eye begins to circle the rim of my glass. He pulls out his iPhone, swipes it open to reveal several pictures of a striking, statuesque black woman who looks capable of catching all kinds of things expertly with her mouth.

"That's my lady." Donny beams. "She's the boss and I like it that way."

"Lovely," I mutter, sinking into the chair.

"Jody's alright," Donny continues, "but he's an idiot. He needs training."

"Training? What is he, an animal?" I can't keep the sarcasm from my voice.

"Yes!" Donny replies. "He's rough around the edges and ugly as fuck! He looks like Gollum from *Lord of the Rings*."

I grimace at that. "You're not exactly being a good wingman here, Donny."

"Ah, he knows I'm only messing. But seriously, Jody, how the hell did you manage to pull her? What did you say to get her down here?"

Jody sticks his middle finger up, smiles. "Charm, something you wouldn't know anything about, you munter."

"How old do you think she is?"

"She won't tell me. She's got a young face but wise eyes. She'd make a good chess player, I'm telling you! And she's Nigerian, you sneaky Russian."

Donny shakes his head. "Be a gentleman. I told you, you

can't tell with black women. Leave it alone."

Jody visibly reddens. "Why not? I told her I'm thirty-eight. I'm no saint, I've done some bad things but I'm straight down the line, me."

"Yeah? And you smoke too much skunk and weed," Donny says.

They go back and forth. I'm amused by their hearty exchange, oddly warmed by the lack of pretence.

"I don't want to find out she's some fourteen-year-old," spits Jody.

"Oh she's not fourteen, Jody, come on!"

They're unaware that the lines in my palms have changed colour, silver in the subdued pub lighting, curling stealthily over the rim of my dwindling glass, or the sand in my zipper. I look up. The Thai barmaid is in the middle of the snooker table, shooting glass mouths into the side pockets instead of balls, Mason is in the TV screen on the football field, legs folded Buddha-style scoffing the rest of his sweets. Several footballers from the game are behind the bar, searching for a ball that went offside an hour ago.

By the time I drain my glass, I hone back into the tail end of the conversation and Donny saying, "She's age appropriate. God! I wish you knew what to do with a woman, you idiot."

I discover several things as time progresses; Jody is down on his luck. He has two kids his ex won't let him see, but he doesn't tell me why. The scar on his neck is from being bottled in a fight by a guy he calls "that fucking all-time loser". He lives in one room, shows me the stitching on his knee from leaping off a wall drunk.

"This is going to be my year, I tell you. Something's going to change. I'm going to grow my own weed in that room, make some money."

There's an urgency in his tone that un-sticks the cork I swallowed from a white wave. I feel it floating between my organs. I recognise the pain in his voice, the fangled thing roaming across his irises intermittently.

He doesn't realise that I have no silhouette. It's not something a person would notice. My silhouette travels through coloured seashells dotted around the city, filled with foreign noises inhabiting it unrepentantly.

Every now and again, he brings the conversation back to his one gripe. "For Christ's sake, will you tell me how old you are?"

I continue toying with him about it. "I'm sixteen," I answer. "I'm carrying my broken hymen inside that rucksack."

"Pfft!" he responds, half-intrigued, half-horrified.

Jody is from a place called Whittington. "It's beautiful, you'd love it," he confides. "My ideal day is at the beach, maybe with a nice lady like yourself or game fishing. I might buy a caravan, travel around. I like the idea of upstarting, you know? Taking old things and revamping them." He sidles up to me; the smell of alcohol lingers on his breath. His eyes are wild, intense. "I'm telling you, Opal, it's going to be my year. Got some family in Australia who know a few people into metal detecting, made a shit load. Might go up there, do that for a bit. Gonna get my kids back." He runs his tongue over his lips. I'm somewhat distracted; lines of sand have made their way onto the pub floor.

In the next hour, Jody explains the difference between sympathy and empathy, calls me a twat for not revealing my age, then apologises since he thought "cunt" was much more offensive. He measures my hands against his, tells me they're older than my face. He's never met his father. His only sister runs a stable.

Midway through my fifth drink, I hold his hand; place my

finger over the pulse on his wrist. "One of these days, you'll go fishing. You'll catch something at the end of the line you never expected."

His eyes crinkle. I feel his heart rate increasing. "You're a funny woman, you know that? Peculiar."

I don't take anything from Jody. After he scribbles his number on a piece of paper, he nips out for a smoke. I head into the toilet, call my friend off a mobile I took from a guy I left in his own blood in an alleyway the night before. He wasn't like Jody. The thing I took from him sat beating at the bottom of my rucksack.

My friend is apologetic about the wait. If someone were to listen in to our conversation, it would sound like static and gibberish. I say goodbye to Donny. Since Jody hasn't come back, I grab my things and slip out discreetly.

Outside, a hollow-faced man is hollering about spotting Jesus holding a pint on the roundabout, a homeless black woman who asks you for money at least three times is being silenced by a blue plastic bag, a cocker spaniel in a priest's collar searches for its saint in dank corners. The dark is sly and full of possibilities. I think of Jody. *This year's going to be my year, I'm telling you.* I think of his moist eyes when he said this, how he seemed to suck the air out of the room.

"I hope so," I say aloud, blinking against the image of him losing his fist in a mouth in the river, a metal detector on his body, unearthing all the hidden things locked inside. I hoist the strap of the rucksack up my shoulder. It digs into my skin, grooves in the cold evening air.

I can feel my gills crying out the alcohol I consumed, shrinking beneath my coat. It's always like this. I talk to them silently. I tell them tomorrow we'll drink water from a bridge, that liquid is coming.

Following

I plucked you from the garden like a root vegetable. A tiny man, you still had soil in the creases of your skin after I dusted you off on the oak kitchen table.

You pointed at me. We studied each other as if we were foreign objects. You spoke in a low, guttural language I didn't understand. Your arms waved at the light breaking in my eyes. I stared at the tiny slit in your miniature penis, growing it with my mouth. The garden door groaned open, a piece of torn, white plastic bag blew in. I remembered the fortune-teller then. I remembered paying for a flower that died on the way back and being handed white seeds after a loaded smile. That night, I'd slipped one seed beneath my tongue and planted the rest, only for things to grow in sleep.

That was three months ago.

Now, you jumped up and down on the table, baring jagged teeth, curling your hands into fists. I hunched down, held a finger to my lips. "Quiet!" I ordered. "Or I'll put you in the freezer for a few hours." You stopped then, understanding my tone perfectly. You smelled of soil and dampness, of things newly born. I pressed my lips to your face, wanting to swallow you whole.

"Bath time," I said, pleasant, almost chirpy. I rummaged through the kitchen cabinets, implosions playing noisily in my head. I filled a deep, plastic bowl with warm water and soaped you down as you wriggled reluctantly.

"Be still," I instructed. Slick from soapy water, you dodged my grasp, settling into sly limbs.

"Bitch! Bitch! Bitch!" you hurled, suddenly speaking English. The words were a rope dangling between my organs. I grabbed you and dumped you in the cutlery drawer, slamming it shut. The clatter of utensils followed me to the sitting room where the wide screen TV waited.

I flicked it on. Images of you rolling between knives and forks interrupted my programmes.

Later, I fished you out. You were bloody and smiling.

"Haha haha. Set me on fire, find the matches." Your grizzly smile stretched, threatening to leave your face. I carried you upstairs, wiped your cuts with cotton wool, watching them become blood clouds in my hands.

At night I plied you with vodka. It was funny to see you stumble around drunk, beneath the cruel glow of flickering candlelight. When you collapsed, I pressed my ear to your chest, comforted by the sound of your heavy panting.

I bought a yellow hamster wheel that squeaked. It sat by the crack on the white window ledge in the bedroom. My eyes returned to it repeatedly, as though it was a small piece of thunder waiting to snag the wheel. Running on that wheel kept you busy and resentful, a tiny fist under the world's crinkly curtain. The sound of turns haunted the rooms. I heard it while drying dishes and polishing cabinets downstairs that housed pictures faced down. It bounced off the thin, silver hands of my leather watch. At times I saw you rushing towards me, waving your fists and talking in another language I couldn't understand. And the wheel had replaced your right leg, squeaking loudly, punctuating the sentences of an unfamiliar language.

The next day, I served you a portion of pasta coated in a wild mushroom and leak sauce.

"Please eat," I said, pushing the saucer of steaming food towards you. Five minutes earlier, you'd torn clumps of matted hair from your head. It lay next to the food as though part of a twisted menu. You took a teaspoon full. I watched your lean, changeable face for approval.

"This isn't very good. I wish you'd disappear." You scrunched your features up. The words formed a stone map in my gut. Later that evening, you ran on the yellow wheel, till it became snippets of a life spinning beneath your feet. The night was a canvass studded with stars, morphing from one day to the next. In its sky, we made love on a knife's edge, blinded by the blood from our cuts.

We sat in my white bathtub under a sea. Above, a man wearing tattered black trousers played the piano, Beethoven's "Symphony 9" to us taking our clothes off. Clothes that became fish in the grip of ripples. A minute or so later, a polka dot fish swam past.

"Sorry, sorry, sorry," you muttered at me as though it was a mantra.

"Why are you telling me this here?" I asked, a naked woman next to a little naked man.

"It's so blue!" you laughed. "Like waking up having a different lens and because things lose their definition here."

Just then, a white and gold packet of Marlboro Lights floated. We took deep breaths, tasting cigarettes on our tongues.

"Well, it's shitty! It's shitty of you to say my pasta wasn't good." I pointed my finger accusingly. It felt like slow motion.

"I didn't say you were a bad person. I said your pasta was average. Sorry you cooked a crappy meal. Sorry, sorry. Sorry."

Mouth over my belly button, you pulled three threads.

The piano man played frenetically. I sensed urgency in his strokes. His reflection was a shimmering looking glass. Your mouth curled over my nipples, sucked gently. The sweet sensation felt like falling into a trap. The bath tub spun away. Fish made from cotton and polyester wrestled things down into the bed of the sea. Only I couldn't see what they were, distracted by tiny tremors of pleasure spreading over my body. The coolness of the water kept me semi-alert. I noticed that the fish were wrestling memories. Images of me laughing on a bridge, dancing in the supermarket aisle, buying a lamp with the half-lizard woman emblazoned on the shade. In each one, the grip of someone holding my hand just outside the frame loosened.

"I brought you here because..." You left the sentence hanging, strung up on the three threads that tugged it away.

"Why are we having this conversation here?"

We came up for air, back in the tub with cold water sloshing down the sides. Our clothes stuck to dimpled bodies. A wooden afro comb had fallen in and was unpicking a tide. I held you in my hands as you tried to scramble off. You were speaking Japanese. And I could have sworn you did that on purpose.

In bed I tossed and turned. I worried about all your possible routes of escape; through a watermark in the bathroom ceiling, hidden in a beer bottle I'd accidentally throw away, disappearing into a pause from a conversation outside.

The following morning at breakfast, you began to speak a language that sounded like Arabic. Crumbs of toast spilled on the table as you talked. You spoke this dialect running up my thighs, eyeing the front door from the thinly carpeted staircase, as if you wanted to squeeze your limbs through the keyhole. You watched my face. I waited for you to walk into my iris and become a tiny silhouette trapped there.

I stuck needles in your skin to silence the noise inside my head. I made you become a doll. When bulbs of blood appeared, I used them to colour the sea beneath a ship I'd drawn.

Days passed, a week became a fortnight and then a month. Our dysfunctional routines continued. I blindfolded you and rammed cockroaches down your throat. Tied you inside bags of rotten fish and listened while you vomited. I stuffed small things inside my vagina, forcing you to find them as I stroked my collarbone. We went out on day trips. You stayed in my pocket on rumbling trains. The feeling of you burrowing reassured me. You tried to grow other heads in there, between the seams and warm lining. I put a stop to that, squeezing them until they disappeared. On one outing to the Science Museum, you spoke in Swahili. I had become used to these random bursts of language and travelling by tongue.

A bank holiday Monday arrived, bright and breezy. In the morning, I found you beside my wardrobe, clutching the leg of a navy pair of men's trousers; tears ran down your cheeks.

I was emptying the bins when you rushed through the half open front door. Horrified, I watched you duck beneath the small, arched gate, past a smattering of cars lining the street and over to the other side. The bins dropped with a thud. My heartbeat quickened. The purple, flannel dressing gown I wore came undone. I was barefoot but there was no time. No time to run back in and grab shoes. I scrambled after you. The warm concrete was hard and unforgiving beneath my feet. You were surprisingly quick. I could just about spot your tiny figure in an ill-fitting tracksuit I'd made, darting into a side path towards the main road. My mouth felt dry and grainy, as though coated in sand.

I ignored the puzzled glances of passersby. I was too busy trying to breathe, to produce a survivor's stroke for an indoor sea that had slipped outside. The smell of carpet pine clung to my nostrils. I stepped on a flattened ginger beer can fleetingly acting as a single shoe. Then, we were both in the wide, slanting road, wild-haired and wild-eyed. I dove to grab you, into the sounds of tires screeching and engines humming like bees. Car horns screamed. The sting from falling on my knees was sharp. I lost my breath to the gaps between the trees. And a big red bus was flying. No. 58. The driver had a blue shirt on. All I could think as you struggled in my hands was *The driver is wearing a sky.*

Inside the kitchen we trembled. I held you beneath a chair leg, hovered it close to your Adam's apple, then grabbed a fork and stabbed it into your thigh.

"Aargh! Please, stop," you yelped, speaking English again.

The piano man played in the distance, on a spiraling, silver staircase. His clothes began to come off, until he was naked. Piano keys uprooted like large teeth as the melancholic tune became more and more haphazard. I started to cry then, because heartbreak smelled like half-eaten rum cake at a breakfast table. I remembered that morning always, you see? The morning you went out for a white and gold packet of Marlboro Lights and never came back. I remembered the agonising wait, months after, knocking our wedding photos face down on shelves and wailing in the musty wardrobe between your clothes.

I turned over my sacrifices as if they were coins. Bits of myself I'd lost in gloves, doorway cracks and printer ink heads. How I'd travelled through echoes, silences, curved fingers over piano keys. All the routes home I'd built for you in the static.

"I'm sorry! *Pardonnez-moi! Kite m'esplike!*" you pleaded, mixing languages as your bottom half began crumbling into bloody soil.

I told you I'd chased your laughter through tunnels and pathways, that I'd been following. And holding the chair leg pressed against your throat, I whispered all the things I'd done to resurrect you.

Mammoth

When the pig's head hit the top of the scale, she threw her arms up in celebration, brown ponytail catching bits of light.

"Can we get ice cream now?"

Perry dropped the mallet, accepted their gift of a slightly dog-eared Daffy Duck from a portly male attendant wearing a red shirt one size too small. His rounded features bore such a distracting sheen, Perry thought they might melt, right into the half-empty bottle of Evian water resting on the prize stand.

"In a minute, Abbie, tie your laces, otherwise you'll injure yourself," he said, adjusting his wire-rimmed glasses around the pink patch they'd cause, that was spreading across the bridge of his nose.

Abbie knelt down, neatly tying her laces, her ten-year-old gangly limbs momentarily curtailed. Already, her blue Wonder Woman t-shirt bore marks. She swiped Daffy from his clutches.

"Will you show me now?" she asked, fidgeting with her gift.

"Soon," he offered, taking her hand. "One thing at a time, honey."

It was a punishingly hot day. The kind of day in which people were advised to stay constantly hydrated, where moments after stepping outside your clothes stuck to your skin.

Seemingly overnight, the sprawling park had been

transformed into a fair. Brightly coloured tents were hives of activity, music boomed from large main stages and the scents of hamburgers and hot dogs filled the air. Fairground rides in the distance were God's toys temporarily on loan. It was so busy, at times you turned and could be swept along the path by a clown on stilts distributing flyers, or a soldier out of uniform eating fire.

Perry spotted the carousel ride seductively glowing in the distance behind a swaying orange tent.

He imagined standing in the middle of the tent as the artificial horses spun around him, above him the sky opening through the orange canvas, multi-coloured scarves falling, weightless, like half-formed wings gently grazing his skin.

As a child he'd loved coming to the fair, which was why he'd brought Abbie there. He recalled his first experience all those years ago at Brockley Park. Standing in awe at the enormous bright tents dotted all over the green, swelling with excitement, threatening to break out onto concrete paths acting as passageways to paradise, people in rides spinning in the volatile sky, ready to become shrunken shrieking things caught by men on stilts if they fell, revelers emerging from the magician's tent as characters they could leave in the gaps of their bedrooms' doors that evening, feeding when necessary. Falling off the carousel ride, looking up at the kaleidoscopic lights in the horses' eyes, watching the sky and their hooves as if they'd come to life stamping on his moist, excitable tongue. He'd wanted to devour it all, experience everything at the same time if he could. He had promised Abbie that feeling. She had told him she needed it.

At the ice cream van, he took the bored-looking owner reading a copy of the *Daily Mail* by surprise when he asked,

"No music?"

The man set his paper aside. Standing, he was almost too tall for the van. He had one blackened half front tooth. His white apron was stained.

He smiled warmly, "Ahh, you mean the jingle. That universal calling card all ice cream vans have."

Perry nodded. "Yes, I've always liked it. It's magical, like a modern day Pied Piper. It's so innocent."

The man chuckled, flipped the freezer behind him open. From the flap, you could catch glimpses of the interior; portable silver compartments, a grey fan, a silent radio bearing flickering red numbers. Perry imagined scenes from the man's life infiltrating the van; a hormonal pregnant wife crying into the ice cream cones, a prepubescent son injuring himself, maybe at football practice, climbing into the freezer to find old injuries stored away. A handful of raucous friends rain dancing around it, the imprint of the steering wheel on a lover's back.

"What will it be for you and your daughter?" The man asked, jarring Perry from his reverie.

"Oh!" He felt his cheeks flushing, embarrassed by his fascination with the lives of others. "Two medium-sized vanilla and uh… flakes too."

Perry caught the man's slightly pitying look at his pockmarked face. It was familiar terrain for Perry, first sympathy then dismissal. The man's gaze flicked to Abbie several feet away. She had shoved her hand inside the duck and was talking to it rapidly, pulling dramatic faces as she orchestrated its responses. Then she rested it on her stomach as though giving it time to breathe, to take in the rumblings of organs raising a quiet alarm.

*

When Perry was sixteen, he volunteered at an old people's home during the summer. It was called Malvern House and sat atop a steep hill, as if the owners not only deliberately made it isolated, but hard to access. A large red bricked building, it boasted a spacious driveway, green grounds, an herb garden and a lake. It sparked the feeling of stumbling into the unknown.

The manager, Mabel, a chubby woman with a permanently cynical sneer, barely peeled her eyes off the paperwork on her desk when he enquired about their voluteering. Indoors, the air was thick and musty. Walls were decorated in dated, flowery green wallpaper. Down the hall, he heard a television blaring from what he assumed to be some sort of common room.

"Shouldn't you be away on holiday somewhere hotter and frankly a lot more interesting?" she closed the file she'd been scribbling in, giving him her full attention. She took in his skinny frame, dank hair and spotty face.

"You don't understand," he said. "This would be a sort of holiday."

"Well, can you do any magic tricks?" She leaned into her chair, studying him carefully.

Perry mostly kept people company. He listened to stories that became grains of sand covering clocks around the building. He took his sketchbook along and captured residents in thoughtful, revealing depictions; Patricia watering her cactus wearing a cowboy hat, Gwendolyn stitching her violet wedding dress, Robert whose Alzheimer's meant he kept scribbled memories in a portable, red phone box, salty from tears.

He directed their proudly OAP production of *Grease*, getting pink and black jackets from local charity shops. Perry felt good inserting himself into their lives, providing some relief. In the beginning, he'd been curious to discover whether life was worth living that long. These people had memories floating within. He kept close, catching them using a discreet, third hand. For two weeks, Robert forgot his goldfish were dead, repeatedly sprinkling food in the glass bowl.

Finally, the ceiling of brown specks shifted, revealing their still, small frames sunk against artificial surroundings. Perry helped groups bake shortbread, sweet buns, soda bread and ginger nut biscuits until he woke at nights unable to get sweet, suffocating smells from his nostrils, violently vomiting in the toilet.

He became friends with a wily character named Monty. Monty was seventy, had haunted, knowing blue eyes and thin, pale skin. He kept a bottle of Appleton State Jamaican rum beneath his mattress; snuck in by a vivacious Jamaican nurse he'd had a crush on who'd long left the care home.

Monty abhorred the staple Sunday dinner of cheap ham, cauliflower, roast potatoes and cold gravy, often declaring, "No imagination! I'd rather eat dog food. Boy, you want to try the steak in Buenos Aires, best ever! And the women… Ah, they'll keep you on your toes." He would stare into the distance, as if the beautiful women had appeared, dancing with his younger self.

Monty never had visitors. He had a son, but their estrangement had lasted years, with no sign of reconciliation.

Perry took to him without knowing why. They played a game of chess that lasted two months, argued over blackjack, raided the contents of the money jar in Mabel's office, leaving Monopoly notes behind instead and bought alcohol with the real money. Sometimes they took long walks on the green, acres the eye drank. Monty would play the blues on his harmonica. He'd get lost in the sound, reaching depths that could only be achieved by playing. He travelled through the instrument, re-emerging bearing John Lee Hooker's right hand.

Once in the herb garden, he showed Perry the spot by the coriander patch where he claimed two members of staff "kicked the shit out of a resident."

"Bastards," he muttered. "I should have taken pictures."

Towards the end of summer, illustrations of Monty in his sketchbook began to fade. His skin became thinner, even on paper. Damp leaves from the winter to come formed small, dull suns in the corners of white pages.

Sitting in the break room one muggy afternoon, watching the generation game, Perry was taken aback when Monty gripped his arm so tightly, red marks appeared. "Will you help me, please?" His eyes glistened. That evening, Monty gave him a shiny, silver watch. "You can sell it, it's worth a bit or keep it if you like."

He did not struggle beneath the weight of the pillow.

For months, Perry thought of Monty playing his harmonica in the garden, where the ducks lost grains of food in shallow unmarked graves. He imagined Monty crossing the shimmering lake beneath a fractured moonlight, before stumbling into the traffic. When he left Malvern House, objects from there followed him; stones, half a photograph, bits of a chintz cushion, like a Frankenstein-formed bird, intermittently swallowing the directions of others.

With a half-smile, he watched Abbie eating pink candy floss by the fortune teller's tent. Out here she projected a pure innocence, a bottomless curiosity, as if life was a series of adventures to be had. They threaded their way through the crowds, catching whiffs of barbecued meat, spicy noodles and an array of other smells. On a park map of scenes seeping into each other they were two small specks.

By the time they left the park that night, sounds from the fair were louder. People could hear it all the way down Pinter Street. Perry had consumed nearly a whole bottle of water to soothe the burning in his throat, to little effect. His forehead glistened. As they crossed the street, Abbie clutched a bag of tangy cola bottles and lollipops in one hand, Daffy Duck in the other. Slightly flushed, she popped one cola bottle into her mouth.

The nondescript white van was tucked away on a quiet side street. They hopped in. As the engine roared to life and The Beach Boys' "God Only Knows" filled the van, Perry whistled along. "You know this song? I love it." He drummed his fingers against the wheel, looking over at Abbie who had a bored expression.

"Can I see it now?" she asked, displaying an impatient pout.

"In a bit."

They drove on the motorway for roughly half an hour before Perry took an exit into an area with gravelly stones that whispered against the tires. He switched off the engine, Perry and Abbie got out and they headed round the back of the van. In the side mirrors, earlier scenes rolled; she and Perry standing outside the park gates, Perry listening attentively as she fretted over handling the blue kite that by now had slotted itself into scenarios with better outcomes.

"Let me see it." Her voice trembled in anticipation.

"Shhh." He placed a finger over his mouth. "I'm showing you."

He opened the back doors. Abbie peeked, but before she could catch her breath he shoved her in, following behind and firmly shutting the doors.

It the dim light of the interior she could just about see the red lacy slip on the floor of the van and the matching lipstick beside it.

Her sweets dropped. The rolling sounds filled Perry's pockets. She picked up the slip, ran a finger over the silky material appreciatively. Slowly she undressed, all the while holding Perry's gaze and the desire she saw in his sad, grey eyes. The Beach Boys' song continued to play on loop. It was the only track on the CD. She untied her ponytail, the loosened hair softly brushed her shoulders. She put the slip on, followed by a slash of red lipstick over her mouth. She placed her hand over Perry's erection with intent.

"Do it," she ordered.

Perry threw her using such force she smacked her head against a stack of windows. Blood dribbled from her forehead.

Perry's artificial moustache came unstuck.

She darted from left to right, dodging Perry's hands, laughing. "Softly, softly catchy monkey," she sang, inching the slip up scrawny thighs.

This was what Abbie enjoyed. She and Perry driving all over the country, taking their private games public, fooling people. For now, she was happy in this ten-year-old body for as long as she needed to see the world through new eyes but when she was done with it, she'd dump it and borrow someone else's body for new adventures.

White noise in Perry's head gathered, separated, indicating the mammoth was coming. Abbie heard it, reaching blindly for Perry, embracing their use of young bodies to deepen their life experiences. There was nothing like it.

Each time that mammoth came, when they had called it with their limbs, it was carnal, necessary and ritualistic. Abbie steadied her breathing, this girl had asthma and the asthma pump she'd kept in her pocket was long gone, borrowed by the marauding baby at the park who was puffing on it earnestly, anchoring itself on her orders. Ahead, illuminated horses from the carousel ride had escaped, eating white road markings. Perry undid his belt buckle and inched forward.

Abbie began to instruct him the way she had the others, across the hollowed silences of indefinable things shrinking into the night.

Vegas

There's a distance in the woman's grey eyes he can't quite identify, that makes a gnawing feeling spread in the pit of his stomach. Officer Philippe aims the torch at her hollow face, which threatens to swallow the light. "Ma'am, you do realise your left taillight is broken? You need to get that fixed ASAP."

The blisteringly hot Nevada desert is only slightly cooler at night; its parched cactuses imitate the silhouettes of men beneath the moon's cracked eye. A tall, strapping figure patrolling the roads, Philippe is almost done for the night. He already tastes a cold Budweiser when he spots the banged-up cream Buick stuttering along and the woman asleep on the driver's side, tawny head bobbing against the wheel.

"Shit," he mutters, before parking his motorcycle beside the now stalled Buick. For some reason, the image of her head bobbing gently made him think of a doll he once found in the river as a boy. And the way ripples ebbed away from its red mouth as if it had been talking to the water's creatures. The woman also has a red mouth which matches her painted toenails. She is barefoot. A gap in her front teeth stirs something in him, making him think of rubbing the slit in his penis there, against another night beyond that gap.

When she finally speaks, she trembles as if her thin frame has already handled too much. "I was robbed earlier, Officer." The voice is paper thin; accent could be from Mississippi, maybe North Carolina; a southern belle. A southern belle vulnerable at the wheel, ready to shimmer away for somebody else to encounter.

Philippe is momentarily distracted thinking about the lines of coke he'd done maybe three to four hours before. He couldn't tell, sometimes he loses sense of time. But he could feel the blood pumping in his veins as she swallows, could hear a shriek in the distance longing to belong, smatterings of light dancing in rear-view mirrors. He could recall his shadow snorting in doorways that were unfamiliar and the lines of the open road dragging him back, limb by limb.

"Are you drunk?" he asks irritably, peering in the darkness of the vehicle, picking up a rotten scent he can't decipher.

Boldly, she grabs hold of his torch. "They took everything, they left me with nothing." A wavering slithers into her voice and she holds the light right up against her face.

There is something so disturbingly bleak about that one action, Philippe can't resist. He yanks the torch back just as a ram's head pops out of her chest asking for his teeth. He blinks the image away, horrified.

She's out of the car now, babbling and unsteady on her feet, rambling about disciples taking her license and registration when she stopped for gas, accosting her out of nowhere like that! He realises she is absentmindedly rubbing his crotch as she speaks.

Other vehicles zip by, a truck carrying bottled water supplies and a fleet of bikers clearly used to minding their business. The sound of their engines ring so loudly in his ears, he feels he might inherit it for a while, feel it revving when his heart stops and starts, when the bloodshot images from his peripheral vision fall out of his eyes as his head thuds on different surfaces, landing with nothing to cushion the fall but the white hot God splintering in his veins. He watches her red mouth, sees it moistened by semen. He knows he will swell and harden in her hold long after she's gone. He knows the cactuses, bored and thirsty, will uproot into the roads and cause accidents.

Later, he drags her into the back seat, takes her roughly, violently. She thanks him for the pardon. Her smile is wide and grateful in the hot air. He doesn't notice spots of dried blood on her thighs.

After he comes, his finger catches in a rip on the hot seat. The smell is more intense now, pungent.

"What the hell is that?" he asks, wondering if she has food stashed somewhere that's gone off. He knows he can smack her head against the wheel repeatedly, watching till it becomes still, just like the doll in the water.

She laughs girlishly. "Oh, that's just Claudine. We're going to Vegas to play blackjack." She yanks her white dress down, clambering into the driver's seat with surprising agility.

Philippe is already turning his lean, handsome face away, as sweat drips into his slanted eyes. There is the sound of something churning, hurtling towards them. And the sky is vast; he is nothing but a tiny thing stumbling from the Buick.

His broken torch has the ram's eye in it glimmering.

He orders her to pop the boot. When she does, he peers into it closely. Something cloaked in bubble wrap catches his eye. He lifts it out gently. It is alien-like. He can see a small hand through the bubbles, a navel, and grey eyes. The rotten stench is unbearable. He wants to cover his nose but cannot do so without dropping it. He removes the bubble wrap, revealing a still baby. The bubble wrap falls, skimming the road. The baby has tiny green veins running across its face, fine tufts of downy hair. He thinks it makes a sound like engine noise, but that cannot be.

Before he can say another word, she hits the gas, tearing

off into the distance at a ridiculous speed with the boot still open. Somebody crazy enough might just leap and land in that opening, in the darkness of the boot and curl into shapes and things that seem impossible. Philippe does not know her name.

He is left holding the dead baby, his flaccid penis hanging obscenely out of his trousers and the night beyond the gap hissing sensuously.

Acknowledgements

A big thank you to my wonderful, kickass agent Elise Dillsworth. Thanks for believing in the work, always having my back and coming along for this crazy ride. Many thanks to publisher and editor Valerie Brandes for guidance and the Jacaranda team for their efforts. Heartfelt thanks to my favourite literary champions; Alex Wheatle for everything and being really inspiring, Yvvette Edwards you are a joyous, magical woman, creative powerhouse Kit Caless for your energy and generous spirit, thanks for all your efforts and support. Thanks to Ben Okri for seeing something in my writing and championing it, Stella Duffy for being open and reading, Rupert Thomson for taking an interest in my work and reading. Thanks to Julian Brown for the years. Thanks to Malaika Adero for publishing some of my work stateside, providing platforms and leading by example. Thanks to David Kwaw Mensah for infectious, endless curiousity about the world around us. Thanks to Rosie Canning and the Greenacre Writers blog team, really appreciate all the support you've given me and so many writers. Thanks to the team at Afrikult, you guys are boss and I love what you're doing. Thanks to Lola Shoneyin and the Ake Festival team for special African memories. Thanks to those wonderful mentors at key stages in my life, Donna Daley-Clarke and Gaylene Gould. Big thanks to Spread the Word, Joy Francis, Words of Colour, Tricia Wombell, Black Book Swap, Zahrah Nesbitt-

Ahmed, Bookshy blog, Samira Sawlani, Media Diversified, Obinna Udenwe for spreading the word about my work on the African blogsphere, Ainehi Edoro, Brittle Paper, Nikesh Shukla and Jon Teckman for the lovely tweets and support. Thanks to London libraries for spaces that helped feed my imagination as a teenager. Thanks to Mum, for all that gumption and always being you, to Dad for the vision, for always being fearless.

About the Author

Irenosen Okojie is a writer and Arts Project Manager. She has worked with the Royal Shakespeare Company, the Southbank Centre and the Caine Prize. Her debut novel *Butterfly Fish* won a Betty Trask Award. Her writing has been featured in *The Guardian* and *The Observer*. Her short stories have been published internationally, including *Kwani 07* and *Phatitude*. She was a selected writer by Theatre Royal Stratford East and Writer in Residence for TEDx East End. She is the Prize Advocate for the SI Leeds Literary Prize. She was a mentor for the Pen to Print project supported by publisher Constable & Robinson. She lives in East London.